T5-AEU-840

WITHDRAWN FROM
KENT STATE UNIVERSITY LIBRARIES

The Love Parlour

Stories by Leon Rooke

For Connie

If Lost Return to the Swiss Arms

He lingered a long time but when the sun was at three o'clock the old man left his place on the park bench and headed for his hotel because by that hour the final mail would have been delivered.

The distance from the park to the hotel was not great but there were some things along the way which the old man took pleasure in watching and today there were some children playing too and because he stood among them until the last one ran home, by the time he reached the Swiss Arms the dinner hour was almost over.

The desk clerk, a young man and his friend, told him the girl was saving his place in the dining-room but that he would have to hurry. This surprised the old man and from his vest pocket he lifted the gold watch, examined it, and with a slow deep breath returned it to his pocket.

"Time certainly flies, doesn't it, son?"

"Yes sir."

"There you go: humouring me because I'm an old man. I know what you're thinking: so young, that you've got all the time in the world."

"You'd best go on in now and eat your soup, sir."

"Soup! It's the only thing I can stand and I can't stand it."

5

He was not hungry but went anyway to his regular table in the corner and sat until he was the last person at the tables, with a cup of tea before him that he did not touch except to put his cold fingers on the warm outside of the cup.

The girl did not come to tell him it was time to close but a short while after that time the old man took the napkin from his lap, gave it a small shake, and returned it to its spot beside the plate. From his change purse he took the dime, placing it on the table with its edge showing from beneath the napkin so that when the girl came to clear the table she would be certain to see it—although the precaution was not necessary since the girl had long since come to expect it there. Of all her tips she valued his dime the most.

Quietly as he had entered he thought to leave the dining hall, to walk swiftly as he could out of the place because he knew that if the girl saw him she would ask why he had not drunk his hot tea or eaten his soup. But this time too she caught him before he got to the door:

"Oh, sir! Sir! You didn't touch your soup and your tea is cold. Why don't you let me bring a tray up to your room later on when your appetite is better? I'd love to do that, if you'll let me."

This she always did. The old man, as he had done so often in the past, told her not to bother, that he felt somewhat tired now and would just like to rest a while.

"Yes, I understand, but I'll just peek in later to see how you feel."

Despite his protests she always brought the tray anyway and sat by it until he ate at least a portion of the food which at one time he would have liked so well but for which he had no taste now.

"Why do you bother with me, an old man?" he asked. "You ought to be giving your attention to that young man out at the desk."

"Oh, he isn't interested in me."

Her eyes flirting with him, she brushed a speck from his coat, gave him a brief, mischievous glance, and left him to clear his table. Such a nice girl, he thought, and watched her until she passed through the swinging doors into the kitchen.

The old man had had intentions of inquiring of the mail when first he returned to the hotel from the park but because the clerk had mentioned nothing about it and because already he had kept them waiting with his dinner he had not asked if a letter by chance had arrived for him. But now he thought he might ascertain the matter and with this in mind he approached the desk.

"Son, did I by any chance—"

The young clerk, smiling warmly, immediately stood and said:

"I'm sorry, sir. I forgot earlier but we're in luck today. A letter came for you."

The old man, who almost never received any mail, told the boy thank you in an apprehensive but eager voice, and watched with some degree of wonder the boy's swift movement as he turned and reached behind him into the narrow box to withdraw the letter. From the clerk's manner the old man knew that he too was happy that a letter finally had come. The clerk passed him the letter then turned away so the old man might regard it with the privacy he desired.

But the old man was perplexed.

"It's typewritten. My name and address, it's typewritten, see here?"

"Yes sir, it certainly is."

Although he didn't say so the old man knew from this that it was highly unlikely that the letter was from any close or personal friend or that it was either of the two letters he had, for such a long time now, been expecting.

"There's no return address. Why is that?"

7

"I don't know, sir. Why don't you open it?"

"What's your hurry? That's what's wrong with you young scamps. Always in a hurry."

"Yes sir."

The old man peered at the envelope a moment longer, then with his penknife he carefully sliced along the end of it. He up-ended the envelope that its contents might slide down but his fingers, cold and crippled, missed the inside letter which slid free and fell to the floor. A second sheet, folded, remained inside.

"I'll pick it up, sir."

But the old man, on guard against that, picked up the letter himself before the boy could pass around the desk. He thought he recognized the letter now, the one which had fallen, and he laid it on the desk and stared at it while fumbling at his breast pocket for his glasses. It was, he knew, his own letter, one which he had composed with great care some time ago and mailed to a lady-friend in another state. But, placing the glasses over his nose, he held the letter at arm's length and, for several moments, studied it.

"She sent it back," he said. "She sent back my letter. Look how ragged it is there where she opened it."

"Yes sir."

"That isn't like her. She must be getting careless in her old age. Wonder why she sent it back?"

"Maybe there's an explanation in the other letter."

"Hmmm. Maybe so, maybe so."

He put that letter aside and picked up the original envelope and blew into it. It puffed open and he pulled from it a folded sheet of white paper.

"Would you like me to read it for you, sir? The light down here isn't too good."

"Yes, yes, that's good of you. I would."

The sheet bore a printed head, proclaiming it to be from

8

the office of the public executor. Below this was the date, the old man's name and address and the words: Dear Sir, Miss Beaumont is—but the boy didn't want to read them.

"Yes, go on, what does it say?"

"It says: 'Dear Sir. Miss Beaumont is dead. She died July 1 of a heart ailment, after a long period of illness. I am hereby returning your letter which was turned over to me with the remainder of her personal belongings."

After some time the old man took off his glasses and fumbled at his breast pocket for his handkerchief. He wanted to wipe the windows of his glasses. But he had forgotten the handkerchief that morning while dressing himself and preparing for his walk to the park. Probably the handkerchief was there now, on the dresser beside the tie clasp which he had also forgotten, and the dozen or so peanuts the counterman at the café had given him days before to feed the squirrels that ran about his feet as he sat on his place on the bench in the park.

"But it doesn't say whether she suffered," he said. "It says nothing."

"I'm sorry sir. Maybe you could write a relative for details."

"Relatives? No. Miss Beaumont was all alone, she had no-one."

"Why not go to your room now and get some rest?"

"Rest? Yes, I'll do that, thank you, son."

"You'll feel much better afterward, I'm sure. I'll have the girl bring you hot soup and—"

"What? Soup? Yes, that would be nice."

The boy ushered him to the foot of the stairs and the old man slowly took them, the letter held loosely open in one hand, his other touching upon the rail. Half-way up he turned: "But she's younger than I am, in perfect health. There must be a mistake."

"Get some rest, sir. You've been out all day."

When the old man had gone safely up the stairs the young

9

clerk went into the dining-room to ask the girl if the old man had eaten properly, and when she said the old man had hardly eaten a bite he said to her that later on if she wished she might take him a little soup and hot tea, that the old man was not feeling well.

"You don't need to tell me," she said, "I was going to do it anyway," and stared at him a moment, not hiding her resentment of his unnecessary suggestion. Abruptly, she whirled and walked away, leaving the boy stranded there wondering why she, mere kitchen help, should always be so huffy with him.

In his room the old man pulled the string that lit the naked bulb above his bed, with one extended hand shielding his eyes from the strong light. He sat on the bed but very soon arose and went to the sink in the corner of the room. He turned on the cold water thinking he might wash his face and rinse the glasses but for several seconds he stood there staring at the running water, his purpose forgotten. He didn't remember to turn off the water but crossed back to the edge of his bed and again sat down. With his fingertips he kneaded the skin around the sunken bridge of his nose, his eyes closed, his head sagging into his shoulders. He rested. He sat a long time that way, then removed the envelope from his pocket, took the executor's note from it, laid the sheet flat on his knees, and read again *Miss Beaumont is dead.* He read the letterhead, the date and salutation and body and complimentary close; this done, he read it again. With a sigh he stretched out over the bed, his hand over his stomach, the letter on his chest. The light bothered his eyes and he pulled the string and closed his eyes to the comfortable darkness. He became aware however of the water pouring from the pipe in the corner and turned his head that way, wondering how long it had been running and if he had turned it on himself. He felt terrible, his body ached throughout, but, shaking his head as if to say that this was only another now-expected barrier thrown up between himself and peace, he rose and walked in his stocking feet to the faucet in the corner.

Once before he fell asleep or as a dream within that sleep he thought of going to the town where Ann Beaumont all her life had lived and where, for a time, they had been the best of friends, to ask of her and to see the grave which claimed her, but that city was a long way and he would not know where to begin and was an old man anyway with only enough money to quietly live out the remainder of his days. Another time, also as if in a dream, he thought he heard the voice of the girl from the dining-room and soon after that the boy from the desk, both of them telling him that here now was his soup and hot tea and that these he should eat and drink if he thought to recover his strength. But then they were gone and he woke up and there was no-one, neither the girl nor the boy, nor soup nor tea either to prove that they had been there, and he was alone. "I feel sorry for them," he thought, "for those two, both of them such fine young people," and thought of them as he dropped off again into sleep, himself hurt in some way he did not understand because although they showed every kindness in the world to him they showed no concern or friendship for one another but a kind of enmity instead which always appeared to grow stronger in his presence.

He did not go to the park the next day but lay stricken in the bed with a great unresolved weight spreading through him, cheered only by the diligent attention of the boy and girl from downstairs.

"I've got to get up from here," he said to the girl that second day. "I can't just lie here and go down with the sun. I've got to get up, get out of this room, go on with my life."

"Then eat your soup," she said, "and be quiet. You fuss a lot to be so young."

"I'm past seventy," he said, "too late to be taking advice from you. What do you know anyway?"

11

"Nothing, perhaps. Except how to cook, how to serve, how to keep an old man from killing himself before he's ready to go."

"That's not enough," he said. "To survive in any kind of style you'll need more."

She removed his dishes, drew the cover up to his nose, and sat a moment holding him in queer regard, squinting, her cheek angled in the palm of her hand. Her elbow rested in her lap, that lively thoughtful expression emerging and receding on her face; she looked, the old man thought, perfectly lovely, bewitching even, strange too, he thought, because he could remember the time when she looked to him like any ordinary girl one might expect to find working on tables in a restaurant.

"You're remarkable," he said, "a remarkable girl. You deserve something more than a job in a restaurant. Keeping tabs on an old man who didn't have the good sense to look after his health. You need a home, a husband and children."

"No thanks," she said, and patted his hand. "Anyway, my job, like my age, is only temporary. I've got to be off now." She rose, straightening from her lap the folds of her clean white uniform.

"You ought to be out chasing after men," he said. "Show that fool downstairs a thing or two." She left, treating him to such a wink and smile that he felt truly cheered, could feel it spreading through him like an instant fluid.

The boy brought the evening newspaper and sat down to read to him.

"Ah, yes," he said, "I know without listening. Someone has called for an end to nuclear testing in the atmosphere, another has called for resumption of testing underground, negotiations lag. In the old days we only flew from New York to Paris and the whole world rejoiced. It was a step forward, a step in the right direction. But what went wrong? Now. . . you ought to pay more attention to that girl, son, she's all you got."

"We're not interested in one another, sir. I wish you would forget all that."

"She's all you've got, and enough too. They've taken the world from you, it's out of your hands now. Listen to this: walk with your good clothes into the poor sections of town and it's only right that they smack you down; walk into the ghettos and if those living there hate you or knock you down that's only right too: a young man, no older than you, told me that only last week, sitting beside me in the park with his dark glasses and beard."

"I don't feel that way."

"You don't? No, I didn't think you did."

"Don't worry about it. You—"

"A man gets my age, you'd think he would know what it's all about. . . . Turn to page twelve. I want to hear what Amy has to say today to BESIEGED, to AT MY WIT'S END."

"I hope you'll feel better soon, sir."

For days the old man lay in convalescence, protesting all the while that he felt no sickness now, that there was no need for this attention, wishing between times for their visits but then telling them when they came they should not trouble themselves so much with him, asking: but what have I to give you? . . . troubled that the companionship he got from them was so much more rewarding than he, old and dull and of no use, could give to them.

"Oh, don't be silly," the girl said, or, teasing, wrinkled her nose at him and said: "Now we don't believe that, do we?" as she ran in on her lunch hour with bright tidy curtains that she had made herself to dress his window; as she dropped in "just for a second" to dust his bureau or with new flowers for his bedside; to freshen his bed or clean the eyeglasses he somehow always misplaced or forgot to wear.

Occasionally, by accident and never by design but just the opposite since the boy and girl tried deliberately to avoid any such encounter, one would arrive while the other also was there, and he would rebuke them with such words as: "I don't know which of you is worse, both of you such nice young people, you could try to find a little happiness in one another," embarrassing each of them to such a degree that one or the other would flee down the corridor.

But then one day she came in and said, "Now, look, you've been playing sick long enough, you can get up now," and he got out of bed and took the chair which she had pulled up by the window with the curtains drawn back, and with the morning sunlight streaming through the window he sat with his head back and the hot bright sun on his face, falling asleep there and sleeping until he woke with lather on his face and the boy asking if he'd like a shave.

"Looks like it's too late now for me to object," the old man said.

"That's right," the boy said, and smiled.

The old man, though saddened by the death of Miss Beaumont and his own failing health, was happy because his young friends treated him so well and began thinking again about getting back into his old routine, the walk to the park that was rich with the sight of familiar people and the loud play of children. After perhaps a week in his room he dressed and went down the stairs. He walked without stopping to see the things he liked normally to watch but went directly to the park, afraid that those in the park might have forgotten him after his long absence. When he had taken his place on the bench they came, the pigeons and the squirrels, but after a while they went elsewhere because the old man had nothing to give them except his time. He felt, despite himself, that things were no longer the same.

"Good morning, Mrs. Knox."

"Good morning, sir. Did you get a good night's rest?"

"Not too well. You see a friend of mine passed on and I—"

"Oh, I'm sorry to hear that, well toodleoo."

"—passed on and. . ."

He was not hungry and did not remember when lunchtime came and passed but was content with sitting and watching the people pass down the paths of the park and the birds drifting from bench to bench where others, old like himself, sat pitching them crumbs.

In the afternoon when the sun was at three o'clock and a shadow half upon the old man's brow he left the park for his hotel, stopping several times on the way to see all that he had missed in those days he had not walked his way to the park. Children were on their knees playing with marbles but the old man's attention was drawn to one in particular and he stopped beside her, fumbling in his pocket for the penny he thought to be there.

"Hello."

"My mommie says I'm not to talk to people I don't know."

The old man watched the young girl streak away from him and a stout woman in blue jeans snatch the child up into her arms at the corner and hurry away with her. The children played on, taking no notice of him. He continued on his way to the Swiss Arms but once within sight of it his spirits began to lift and he was happy to see the clerk coming through the lobby toward him and pleased as the boy lightly touched his elbow and led him to his place in the dining-room.

"I'll sit with you a moment if you don't mind," the boy said, and sat down opposite the old man at the small table. "How was your day, your strength coming back?"

"Fine, fine," the old man said, meticulously spreading the napkin over his lap, embarrassed then and resisting the desire to advise the boy he should not snap his fingers that way and stare off so impatiently at the girl busy at another table, that there was no hurry, she would get to them when she could.

"There's no reason for this," the boy said, waiting a moment longer, and the old man, watching the boy, began to see that the enmity between the two was stronger now and puzzled over the cause.

"She has instructions to serve you immediately when you enter," the boy said, "I told her so myself."

"That wasn't necessary," the old man began, "she—"

"I know she's your friend," the boy said, "but she doesn't take her job seriously, she thinks she can sing her way through anything, she doesn't do what she's told, she isn't even nice."

The old man thought this all so absurdly untrue that a smile grabbed at the corners of his mouth and he looked off apologetically at the girl. Catching his eye, the girl smiled too which the old man acknowledged with a slight dip of his head, but with his back to the girl the boy was unaware of the exchange.

"Excuse me," the boy said, "I'll see what I can do," and he angrily rose from the table.

"Please," the old man said, "there's no need, no need to get upset."

But the boy already was going, trailing after the girl who now was hurrying through the swinging doors of the kitchen with a tray of soiled dishes in her hands.

"Don't, please," the old man said but by the time he got up both were out of sight. He followed to the swinging doors but stood there perplexed, debating whether he should intrude, if already he had not intruded too much into their affairs. From where he stood he could hear them, their voices crossing one another's speech, their imposed hush intensifying that anger all the more, among their words his own name, not his name either but *the old man*, the girl saying *You've been waiting for this along time haven't you?* to which the boy was replying *That's a lie, not me but you,* and more of it until at once it struck the old man that in no uncertain way he as much as anything was the cause of their animosity, that odd as it was one was angry at the other for the attention that other was showing him, that they were jealous of this attention but he couldn't believe this and stood as before debating whether he should intervene, stop their argument, tell them how it pained him to see them this way.

If only he knew you as you really are, the boy was saying.

Which way? the girl answered. *How would you know how I really am or anything about me, why are you such a fool?*

Me!

Yes, you! a fool! And the sharp crossfire continuing as the old man turned away and with his slow stiff steps left the room.

Later when the girl climbed the stairs with his hot soup and tea she found his door locked and no answer to her call and later still when the boy tapped on the door and said that he was going off duty now and was there anything he could do before he left he got no reply either although both had the feeling that he was in the room and deliberately refusing them.

The next day the old man was up early and out of the hotel before the boy gained his station behind the desk and neither saw him until evening when he took his seat well within the dining-room hour. He said nothing when the girl told him that she had missed him and commented that he seemed a little tired, and although it pained him to treat her with such indifference, confused over what he ought to do, shortly thereafter he replaced the napkin on the table and left the room.

"That man," the girl thought when she came to clear his table, "he eats nothing, how does he live?" and she thought of him with much concern and even love, like a father he was, a *dear* old man, but when she lifted the napkin and reached for the customary dime it wasn't there. No, she thought, of course it's here, and she pushed aside the plate but it wasn't there and she opened the napkin thinking the dime might have caught in a fold but it wasn't there. He had not left it.

She ran to the desk and told the clerk: "Something is wrong, he always leaves it," but the clerk was insistent: "No, it probably slipped his mind."

"That isn't the case," she said, "I know it isn't, something is wrong."

The clerk himself went into the dining hall to look but found nothing and returned to find her standing at the foot of the stairs looking up toward the old man's room.

"He's been acting strangely since yesterday," the girl said, "did you say something to upset him?"

"Me? No, why should I?"

"Because you're so ignorant," she said, "you wouldn't know even if you had," and at that the boy stared hard at her, frustrated by her reasoning and hating her for her arrogance.

"If you're so smart," he said, "why don't you do something to help him, why don't you leave him alone?" and the girl opened her mouth in a kind of amazement and gazed at the boy and he gazed back until she said, "Oh, you're so silly, so very silly," and turned her back to him and escaped into the dining-room.

In his room the old man lay on the bed, his hands clasped over his stomach, his eyes closed before the glare of the naked swinging light above. He felt in his breast pocket for his handkerchief, thinking to use this as a shield for his eyes, but his pocket was empty. He fingered his vest pockets too but found in one only his gold watch and in another the hard remains of breadcrumbs saved from a lunch he did not recall. If he had remembered he could have tossed these to the pigeons but he had forgotten them as so often he had forgotten the electric light and the water faucet and the names of the boy and girl downstairs who had been and were still so nice to him. He didn't notice the handkerchief on the bedside table nor did he at first think to pull the string that would turn off the bulb. When finally he did, the room was pitched into such breathtaking darkness that the old man felt a strange feebleness, worse than his sickness; he felt his own loneliness and inefficacy. He longed for the quick impulsive smile of the girl, the serious, sulking figure of the boy. He pulled on the light again and lay staring up at the bright dusty bulb. Without turning his head he could see cobwebs in each corner of the room and the broken plaster in the ceiling. "It's a clean hotel," he thought, "how did they get there? Every minute of your life you're pushing one way and something else is pushing another, and how is it that you know when to stop pushing? It's such an effort," he thought, "such an effort to get along"—but this was self-indulgence, he felt, an old man's effort to reconcile his sad ending with his ill achievements, and to avoid such thoughts he rolled on his side and held that position until the wall fell away and he found sleep.

Later on the boy knocked on the door and, getting no answer, let himself in. "Just like a girl," he thought, "to think the worst. The old man is fine, he's sleeping," and quietly he closed the door and went downstairs.

But the girl was worried and afraid and when she came with his tray of food and got no answer she stood a long time outside the door with her legs apart and her head down, much as if she could feel through the door the great fatigue which she fancied he must be feeling.

When the light of the morning sun broke through the curtains the old man awoke. He scolded himself for having left the electric light burning through the night and for having gone to sleep in his clothes. Now they would have to be pressed, another expense. He wondered what time it was and why he had done such foolish things and he stared a long time at the dust particles suspended and turning in the funnel of sunlight that flooded the window before he remembered that his long-ago friend was no longer alive. He wondered too what the cause was and was touched with the fear that not knowing the cause was somehow his own fault and he felt guilty too to recall that there had been times in the last few years when he had envied her, thinking surely that she, being so charming and so *good* a person, would have more than an abundance of friends and diversions.

He sat throughout the morning in his room, remembering Miss Beaumont, considering himself, as he stared at the dust particles treadmilling up from the floor along that bright beam of sunlight, realizing too that the dust existed outside of that beam as well, that all over the room, unseen, the dust was moving, wondering why in a room so still this should be so.

He left his room and went down the stairs and through the lobby and walked outside and gained a chair on the lawn, turning it away from the sun. Although he expected no more letters he thought to wait for the postman who might after all bring a circular or two. No, no letters. All his old friends were gone, forgotten, had drifted beyond all knowledge of him; he sat on, rocking, waiting. He wanted to walk to the park, there to sit and feed and watch the birds and squirrels but he had nothing to give them and not the strength to get there. A mother with her two boys and a girl crossed by him on the sidewalk and he gazed at them but they walked on, chatting, taking no notice.

Somehow he missed the postman. He woke, with a snap of his head from his shoulders, and knew that it was late. Cold. He arose from his chair and entered the hotel and began climbing the stairs to his room. But he had forgotten his key. Standing before his door, fumbling idly in his pockets, he tried to recall where he had left it, the key attached to the small diamond-shaped plastic holder which had impressed on it the words IF LOST RETURN TO THE SWISS ARMS. He was about to return to the lobby to ask for the duplicate when he saw the clerk bounding up the stairs, bringing it.

"Lost it again, huh?" the clerk said, and smiled. He opened the door and stepped aside for the old man to enter and then he entered himself. Once again the boy was struck by the peculiar odour and order and particular shade of everything in the old man's room that pastel curtains alone could not dispel. The overhead light was burning and he reached up and quietly pulled the string that put it out.

"I think I'd like a little taste of something to eat later on. Will the girl be coming up?"

"Yes sir, I'll see about that, you just take it easy."

"She's a nice girl."

"Sir?"

"A pretty little thing."

"Yes sir."

"Such a nice girl."

"She likes you too, sir."

The boy could see that the conversation tired the old man, that he was pale and had no strength, and suggested that he go to bed but the old man sat on, gazing out of the window, hardly aware that he had been spoken to. Leaving, the boy silently closed the door.

A great pain struck the old man soon after the boy had gone and he struggled to the bed and sat on its edge waiting for the pain to quit but the pain remained and the old man lay down, watching the ceiling and thinking that this pain, with a life of its own, might reach out and touch him anywhere.

In the evening the girl brought the tea and the soup and sat with him urging him to eat it, that he must, falling silent when the old man could not.

"I'll be all right," he said, "you go on back to your young man."

"He isn't my young man," she said.

"Go on back to him."

"But I'm not interested—"

"*Listen to me!*" he said, and she fell silent, sensing the urgency in his voice, waiting for him to continue, but finding just that urgency there, nothing more, as the old man blinked his eyes and rolled his head from side to side, blinking his eyes as the pain rolled with him.

"Do something," he said, "don't let it slip away like this," and in the corridor outside his door a few minutes later the girl thought about and tried to scramble some sense into his words: that vague *something* and *it*, he had said, but of what *it* was he speaking? Life? Probably so but if so whose had he meant: his own? Hers? The young man's? But the question was passed over quickly by the weight of her remorse: the old man was suffering, he would need a doctor.

The doctor after much persuasion came and examined the old man in his room and after a brief probing told them all that there was nothing wrong, that the old man had another ten or fifteen good years left in him, that he should rest and sleep and avoid any excitement and the doctor was paid and he left.

"See, I told you," the boy said to the girl, "there was nothing to worry about."

But the girl was not convinced.

Much later that evening a taxi stopped before the hotel and the girl emerged from it and told the driver to wait and she went into the hotel. She wore street clothes, the lamb's wool sweater and the stylish skirt on which she had spent a large portion of her salary; she wore heels and brought in her purse the present for the old man which she had got from the drug-store. In his room the old man was at a loss for the words by which to express his thanks or his regrets but at the same time he felt a heavy impatience; the girl's face reflected her own doubts but the old man read determination and understanding there too and he tried bravely to stifle his pain until she had gone and when she bent over and kissed his brow and said she was leaving now he told her that her lips were warm like the sun, which brought the trace of a smile into her eyes and when he said that she must get back to her young man now she said yes, I'm going and like that she left his room.

Downstairs, she paused at the dining-room entrance and looked in and stood a moment undecided before she entered and went directly to the old man's table and removed the RESERVED sign from it and walked out and got into her taxi and was taken away from the Swiss Arms hotel.

In the night the old man died. He died quietly, with his hands across his chest, the overhead light burning and the water running in the faucet at the corner.

Leave Running

You awake, Igor? Igor?

By her side Rose's lover stirred.

Igor the thief, Igor the lover—opened his eyes, saw the sun sliced on the floor.

God, don't you hate Venetian blinds?

It wasn't the blinds but the sun that Igor didn't like.

Cigarette, Igor?

Her finger poked his shoulder. Poked again.

Igor?

You know, Rose, said Igor—Rose, you know I never smoke.

No, she said, I didn't know. She poked again but he refused to move. Igor, thief and lover, refusing to turn and look at her.

I've got to go.

He said nothing. She saw him close his eyes, and immediately her own eyes were shut tight.

Flesh is impermanent; let us grieve that it is not forever anchored to these beds. To these afternoons. She lifted a thin arm as if to compel the Venetian blinds to close and descend.

I've got to, she said.

Go, he said.

People of Igor's persuasion are trained for this. They come and go, they enter and leave. What they find in between is all the burden that they have.

She rested on an elbow—surveyed Igor's room. Drab, sterile, empty—she would find no ghosts here. Her fingers stroked lazily through Igor's hair.

All my life people have been leaving me or I have been leaving them. Parents, children, friends. My husband goes to work, my children go to school. Where did I go, Igor, before you came to me?

Igor groaned.

What are you looking at, Igor?

The floor.

She placed an ear against his lips to get these words. Igor the house thief, Igor the break-in man: it was not his habit to speak often or loud. He adjusted his voice only to compensate for whatever noise was occurring within. Within himself, that is, where stealth was the rule. Igor spoke the way he moved: a shadow at the back door. Lift a latch, slither through. Igor the cat burglar is inside your house. Hide your silverware, your TV, put a lock on your bedroom door.

Rose shifted, rolled away from him. His skin was damp, he looked too thin, too dirty. The smell of the thousand closets and basements he had hidden in, passed nights inside, attached itself to him.

(One night you awaken, your husband is asleep by your side, you hear a creak in the floor—and there in the dark stands Igor the housebreaker at your husband's dresser, dousing himself with cologne. You watch his face in the mirror; minutes go by before you realize he has also been watching yours).

I smoke too much. I know I do. Maybe I shouldn't have come.

Maybe, he said.

Across the line of shotgun rooms a grueling trail of abandoned clothes. The afternoon had a weight Igor couldn't endure. He needed night. Darkness. Then he could slither free.

She fussed, blew smoke across his nose: You're no help at all. In your own way you're just like Talbert. Next time I'll send him. Maybe you'd like that.

Igor lay very still. This woman frightened him. People did who didn't know when or how to shut up.

(She had sat up in bed that night and said, Try the *Monsieur de Givenchy*, it's the best in the house).

She stared at his sunken cheeks— Igor, why don't you ever shave?—at his pale flesh, his bones, his thin chest and dirty nails—at the stubble of beard which was blue. Her own cheeks burned.

I get along.

Igor resented this. This woman was silly, it was not her business to instruct him. He could ask questions, too: why have you been following me? What is your purpose with me? But he knew the answers: Rose wanted to be the housebreaker now.

I do okay.

Yes, she said. Her wine-red nails traced along his spine. Yes, I'm sure you do.

He burrowed deeper under the sheet. His rooms held no secrets, contained no evidence; they were furnished as they had come. The rooms to his mind, were a mark of pride: anyone could live here.

Igor, you don't have to continue in this line. I have money enough for the two of us.

She lifted the sheet off him.

It may be a low-risk profession, she said, but you could still get caught and go to jail.

Igor thought it unlikely. Houses didn't resist; their occupants didn't either. They watched TV, they read, they slept. Wall-to-wall carpets cushioned his steps. He rarely had to search for what he came for. In fact, it seemed to Igor that these houses welcomed him.

(That night she had let her husband sleep. Had made no move to reach the bedside phone. Had left her body exposed.

Do you like the *Givenchy*? Talbert's wallet is in his inside breast pocket. Did you find my jewels?

Of course he had fled. And although he had taken a circuitous route in returning here—darting up alleys and across back yards—he had sensed someone in pursuit of him.)

After all, Igor, it isn't especially ennobling to be what you are. To steal from people you've never seen. What did you do with our toaster? Two bucks at a pawn shop?

Igor remained silent and still.

Igor? Igor?

Her voice was a whisper. Igor, listen! Did you hear something just then? Has someone broken in?

The woman was silly; she was playing games. But he turned, looked at her.

Igor? When you go out tonight, I want to go with you.

He shook his head in protest. His fists gripped the sheet.

I'll be careful. I won't even enter the house with you, I'll stay outside and watch, if that will make you more comfortable. But I want to see the house you rob. I want to be there when you break in.

She stretched across him, reaching for the ash tray, raking his face with her breasts. He caught a nipple in his mouth, closed his teeth on it. He bit hard—harder; she held her breath, pressed against him.

Harder, Igor. Harder.

Her expression never changed. Finally he let go, licked gently around the wound.

That hurt, Igor. But I have control. I can be quiet. I can walk on cat feet. They will never know I am there. Which house do we hit, Igor? Have you one picked out? Can we do it tonight?

Good second-storey men do not take disciples on. Do not

conduct tours for women who have nothing else to do. It takes one man alone to feel out and come to terms with that darkness in which people live.

Take me with you, Igor.

The risks were increasing. Around him, Igor suspected, traps were being laid.

No, Rose. Rose, go home.

At home—at home her husband Talbert was swearing at the piled-up sink, the filthy house—mess of scabby wounds over every minute of this and every other bleeding day. What a goddamn day, where is she? Where? Where are you, Rose? He stormed from kitchen to living-room to bathroom door: stood there pounding on the painted plywood. Nell? Rose-Nell, you in there? I'm coming in! He waited, hearing her scream *don't you dare*; her quick urgency as she flushed the toilet, closed the lid, stood to face him, scowling, near to tears: "Can't you see it's occupied! Must you always barge right in!" He opened the door to the empty room—to this room empty as every other.

Another indignity spared.

But where are you, Rose?

The floor showed pools of water by the tub, bathing accoutrements overturned. Careless, arrogant Rose had had occasion to wash herself, she could not be bothered to pick up or even to rearrange her debris: oils, milk bath by Xanadu, her Jean Naté lotions, her talcum by Shalimar. Wherever she was she'd be smelling good. Too goddamn good, he thought, cursing her for that part she had left him: tiny dark leg-hairs at the bottom of the tub, his razor on the ledge unclean. Bitch, he said—flipped on the tap, washed the Gillette clean. The water pipes clanged, nothing in this house is worth a damn.

He turned, followed over the waxed floor a wet trail of feet —entered the bedroom. The closet was open, wire hangers scattered about in a tangle—like live things, he thought, thin idiotic little bastards that had fought among themselves. Clothes had slid free, frothy soft piles of cotton, satin, velvet, acrylic nothings now a rummage load, mummy wrappings above her unmatched shoes. One of the four sliding doors slammed off its rollers: further evidence of flight. And now, here, another pool of water where she had sat at her dressing table preparing her Bitch-Mother-Goddess face.

Lousy bitch, fucking Mother-Goddess face. He sat on her wet, padded stool, studied his own mirrored face. In the old days there might have been lipstick messages on the glass: GONE TO SCHOOL, GONE TO STORE (DINNER IN THE FRIDGE). Civilization, he thought, what place have we come to now? With the coming of streets, housing tracts with scrub-yards, the pouring of concrete over every falling mile—with all that, a man could no longer track another human down. All the tracks covered over. They sped from here to there—suburb to city—somewhere in between they disappeared. Carried there —Nell anyway—by salmon instinct, by whatever else was blind in them. . . to run against the stream a thousand miles, back to place of birth, back to whatever had spawned them, there themselves to spawn, mingle bodies, mingle ocean oil and Georgia Strait perfumes: plant eggs, rot and die: float on the reeking surface of those polluted creeks and streams the little hatched ones can't flee from fast enough.

Nell?

Rose-Nell?

He sat there calling her name, he didn't know why.

Stupid, he said. Out of my goddamn head.

On the strewn bed the clothes she'd contemplated and refused. In an age of abundance looking for the one pure dress, the one perfect garment for her much-considered flesh.

Zipper me up, Talbert.

Talbert, don't sit here sulking, dopey as a mule.

He leaned, lifted organdy frock to hand, buried his face within its folds. Powder, sweat, mold, perfumes: that good closet mulch. Here a stain under the arm, let's throw this one aside. Now another—but no good, observe the broken stitch. Try this one, yard upon yard of see-through Turkish stretch, painted eyes here where breasts would rise. A gift, he remembered, of Christmas last, a small offering intended to ease the strain of times too hard: themselves at each other's throat. Something whimsical and sexy from him to her, notice that hereafter he would try harder to satisfy. With it a card written in Santa's hand: WHEN YOU WEAR THIS HOW CAN I REFUSE? Yet he had, not once but a dozen times. With her clothes off she scared him half to death, another bloody perfect body saying *Satisfy, satisfy!*

He pitched it down. $70 at Mr. Pearl's Main Street store but not good enough for whatever she was doing now. Fucking bitch, the feather-footed toad! For a month now he'd come home to find her in blue jeans, ratty knees and drooping seat, ratty bandana holding up her dingy hair—up to her ears in smoke, in a litter of tea cups and her ratty magazines.

Good day? he'd ask.

Up yours!

What had happened to his perfect bride?

Igor?

She rolled, stubbing out her cigarette. Hating cigarettes, her menthol mouth. One day I'll put an entire package in my jaws, chew on that: get my fill of the bloody things.

Watch it, he warned—but too late. The tray overturned, scattering ash and stub over Igor and the sheet.

I'm sorry, she said. Clumsy. Maybe I'm nervous. Why don't you wash this filthy sheet.

She fingered ashes and cigarettes into a pile, then placed the ash tray upside-down over the imperfect mound.

Now they're safe, she said. And smiled for the very first time that day. Do you enjoy me, Igor?

He shifted, wanting to put space between himself and her. Stroking her buttocks with one light hand while the second stroked to find that shape in the air.

The chemists are wrong. Air is composed of solids—they are invisible but they are there. Ask any break-and-enter man; it is the first lesson learned.

God, he said, don't you hate Venetian blinds?

He stared gloomily at the floor. Was the sun going down? The window's shadow still angled along the floor, sun slicing through the open blinds. But the blades were less distinct now. Shadows were in retreat. Soon the night would conquer all.

A few theologians are on the right track; soon night will be all there is.

I notice nothing about these rooms, Igor. I couldn't tell anyone what this place looks like, even at the threat of death. The police may wring my neck, they'll get nothing out of me. Do you have any chairs? Rugs? Is that a linoleum floor? What colour are your walls? I don't know, Igor. I don't know an Igor either. What was that name again?

In Igor's view, she talked too much. She would want to wake her victims: Hello. Igor and I are burglarizing your home.

She might even be violent, for all he knew. Would looting be enough? Women who behave like this can kill. He could see her shaking her victims awake: Hello. I'm stabbing you now.

Igor, do you know what I'm looking for? In those houses I hope to enter with you?

Igor shook his head.

Sure. A marriage better than your own.

At home her husband Talbert sat at her dressing table, balanced on the padded mahogany stool. Another antique, he thought, like myself. He stared at the mirror, said out loud: I see you, Talbert. And leaned close, intending to determine if indeed there were something or someone there:

The person I was, he meant, before I became me.

Good eyes, he said, I see you. I can look into them and believe I exist. But it was because he could remember the good old days—when he had believed. He settled back, crossed his legs. Fusing within his, her image too.

Where are you, Rose.

A cold dampness on his lower back made him twist about: her abandoned towel, pressed flat now, marring the finish of this ridiculous stool. Inlaid silver no longer gleamed. Four hundred dollars, just six months ago, at the Antique Gallery on Fort Street.

In this house, he thought, the furniture has value but that's all that does. He could place these antiques end to end and they'd reach all the way out of town. But all the way wasn't far enough. What am I doing here? Why do I bother to come home? He didn't know. Time had him floating here. Up the old river looking for his pretty salmon mate. Time would float him on again. Vaguely, he could remember it had been a busy day. His days always were; it is out of jealousy that the night has a thousand eyes. He got up, kicked the stool, balled a fist, stuck it to the mirror's nose: Up your ass, mirror! He turned and left the room before his venom could mellow into disgust.

The children had come in. In the TV room they didn't look up as he passed—slouching, lingering—by the door. Children, he thought, *my* children! Gloomy lamp-post sons. Do you see me here? Your old Dad? Scratch gravel, Tonto, hi-yo Silver, awayyyyyyyy! What I had only on Saturday afternoons, they now have every day. I resent that, yes, I do. His own childhood had been lived in a wait for Saturday, for the afternoon western, for the evening horror show. Occasionally Frankenstein and the Wolfman still moved behind this glass but the horror had gone out of them and left nothing in its place.

Fucking TV, he muttered, and kicked the wall. Walked on. You, Talbert, are the monster now.

The metal clamour, metasonic boom, rang in his ears, pursuing him back to the kitchen where he rattled pots and pans, searched for a dish towel that didn't have the stench of decaying food. Liberated womanhood had saddled him without fanfare to house and stove. Pick up, scrub up, hurry up—dump all your garbage, Talbert, into this pail. Then dump pail over the TV, over the rabbit ears, over your rapt-eyed sons. Here's advice, sons: swim into the canned laughter, the metered applause, join ranks with the garbage men.

Goddamned stove. He swiped damp cloth around the metal rings. Around the drunken metal eyes. Slapped it across the enamel top. Stooped—flushing, hurting in his joints—and smeared away at grease, coffee stains, blood—this anonymous scum. Stood and slowly wiped the metal eyes again. Through these eyes one saw into the soul of this Hotpoint stove, these eyes that could work man or woman into an early grave.

Something is wrong with us. It is madness to insist on three meals each day. Or even two. The cattle should eat us. That would change our habits quick.

He turned on the electric eye, watched it go red. What are you doing, Talbert? I am working in a circle. You start here and slowly close it around. At this moment you are about at this point and as you can see, Talbert, things are heating up. We call this, Talbert, the story of your life.

He turned off the stove. Watched the eye go cold, and nodded his appreciation: either way it was the story of his life.

Where are you, Rose?

The kids would have to be fed soon. Kids have no dignity, they scream when they are hungry. His had been taught to scream three times a day. Conversations with his own mother came back to him:

33

What would you like for dinner, son?

A bleeding field of sugar cane. I want to chomp into a bag-ful of clouds, to chew them and swallow them and float away to be broken up and blown and made to fall again like rain.

You're a shitty little son, his mother had said, why don't you go off somewhere and play with yourself?

A bold, beautiful, prefab woman. She would fold tent and go, flee living better than any other living thing. Snotnose. Dirty face. Your father was a Jew, him I have to thank for this.

Well better him, she said, than you! His mom: ironing in the raw, pointing her iron at the three weeks' growth of beard, the three weeks of fermenting brew who sat at the table oppo-site them, elbows at rest among apple peels, showing apprecia-tion in his teeth. Jawing death, his mother would have said.

Oh your mom's a devil, isn't she, son! If God hadn't been tired He'd have worked on her some more.

He? Who is the *He* you're speaking of? Stuff Him up your big Jewish nose. Screw, Mama said, your old hook-nosed God! And circled the table, leaving the iron to smoke away the iron-ing board—leaving all to bend and stick her mouth on his, poke her tongue inside, working to open his fly and place her hand inside.

But I love the big Jewish prick!

Dear old mom: she knew how to keep a boy on his toes, knew how to make those close to her stop and think.

You go on about your business, said mom. Can't you see your father and I have business here? Come on, pa—awake!

He applied a last dab of filthy cloth to the laminated counter top: waited a moment, fascinated, as the wet trails dried, leav-ing nothing there. Except himself and pa and dear old mom. He turned, flung the grimy crumb-sodden cloth across the room to the piled-up dishes in the sink.

Wash yourselves.

Then strode back through the dining-room, the living-room,

bedroom, sunroom and hall—making the rounds like a night watchman with a watch on everything but his clock. Wrestled back to the TV door and yelled:

You fucking kids! You dope-eyed kids, turn off the set! Off! Get your sad tails outside! Go on, go! Outside and play! Take your baseball hats, your hockey sticks, your skates, your goddamned—

Aww, Dad, moaned the oldest—we want to see the end of this!

Of what? Do you even know what you're watching?

It's Gilligan's Island, Dad. They've found gold!

Marooned, marooned. Let myself be marooned like that silly ass, Gilligan: rewound, rerun, to find gold here at five o'clock with these bloody kids. He relented, standing before them with twisting torso, his insides knotting hard—then took a deep breath, kicked air, kicked at Gilligan's imbecilic face— kicked at them. No, no, get your tails outside and play, I mean it now!

But, Dad.

Don't Dad me and where's your Mom?

The boys raised cherub chins, see-through cherub eyes. Eyes mirthless now but void of any chagrin.

How should we know?

You accuse us falsely, oh the injustice of it, Dad! They eased themselves out of the room, tracking lightly around his fumes. Trekked toward the front door, looking over their shoulders —gave a single anguished cry, and disappeared. Consumed by space, vanquished—banished—gone into thin air. Silence, a silent flesh-eating house. Blessed lovely silence, blessed, so rare as to make him believe for a moment that he'd never known such silence before. Since before his marriage, before his birth —before he became an egg warming himself here in the lower depths of this salmon pool. Before. . . he stopped, had caught a flash of arm—heard a giggle now. A shoosh.

35

He'll hear you. Don't make a sound.

The boys had snuck back through to kitchen, dirty sneaking Beelzebubs. . . back there piling jam, cheese, butter, peanut butter, ice cream and frozen steaks between their slices of Melba Toast. Munch and crunch on it, root sodas out of the refrigerator, guzzle beers—gargoyled little runty bastards who never could get filled.

Eating me out of house and home, out of my frozen steaks.

Passing time, goddammit, until they could sneak back in here, match wits with Gilligan the fool. Thieves, skulking natives, smartass idiot sons.

Nell's perfect darlings.

He turned on the TV, sat down himself. Stretched his legs. The image blurred, would that it would ever so remain. Retreated, reappeared. This brainless comedy. Marooned between toothpaste ads, between utter stupidity and total insanity—halfass Gilligan now monkey-struggling through the brush, having lost the pirated hoard once found. Dung, dung, said Talbert.

Oh God, what manure!

Is this why Nell had escaped the house? Why she dunged herself out in fine dress and monkey-perfume? Who could blame? A smart woman, Rose. He kicked at Gilligan, aiming for the crotch—succeeding only in jostling the set. Gold glittered in three tides of Quasar green. He took off his shoe, set foot to rest against Giggigan's—Gooligan's?—Gangugee's?—monkey jaws. Did Gilligan have a wife? A child somewhere?

Do you know where they are?

Canned laughter erupted from the set, swimming up his leg, into his head. A drink, I need a drink, he said. A shot of your best magic, doctor, shoot it to me in the veins.

He remained seated, lacking the wherewithal. Good old-fashioned wherewithal. His eyes ached. His very goddamned eyelids ached.

My very goddamn eyelids, doc.

Igor?

She thumped her cigarette, letting the ashes fall on him.

People are nicer when they're happy. Igor, let me come with you?

She held the hot tip of the cigarette an inch above his skin.

Igor, I'm warning you.

My very goddamn eyelids, he said. Outside—outside he heard a car breezing past, screech of tires, horn raking the neighbourhood. Goddamn horn, goddamn neighbourhood—what was it this time, who were they looking for? He struggled up, stumbled to the window, peered through. Nell?

It didn't sound like Nell's car but was it Nell?

Rose-Nell, have you come home? Back to people who love you?

But it wasn't Nell. Down the street a boy in a hard hat sitting easy at the wheel of an open yellow Porsche—back from the squandered dead, back from the rotting heart of the city to look up old school chums, to say Chums, that's how it was. To roll back the sleeve, spit on the needle, say Shoot it to me, Chums, right here. Talbert flipped the curtain aside, flexed his muscle, stared at his trembling arm.

This one's a downer, doc, the fish can't get up this stream.

He went back to the window, crazy nosy old bat with one shoe off and one shoe on. Down the street at the house where the Porsche had drawn up, romped a long-haired giggling girl, arms performing a flute dance to the honking horn—now hitting the street in hiphugger boots, tassle-strung leather coat, a shriek that split his ears. She hurled herself across the car's low-slung hood, the driver slid low, geared, spun tires, shot off with the speed of a killer whale.

Praise Love, young love, thought Talbert—Old Burp Gun,

37

Burp God Love, mother of us all.

Nothing like a hot date with a man who knows his wheels.

He wrenched back to his chair, kicked horizontal bars out of the TV face—sat down. Oh to be down on the street, to be off and away, with such an ornament on my hood. To have this instead, this orbit within the Burp God womb, to feed on pep pills, supermarket fluff and bleach, the usual piss politics. To be ever within arm's reach of war, six million Jews, Fascist pigs as heads of state, snipers in the tower, madmen in the trees, how many crazy C. Mansons Mylaiing how many other poor sonsofbitches in how many other villages all along the trail. All along expressways and byways, from the heart of the city to the heart of the city dump.

Nell, Nell, I need you, Nell!

Dad, Dad, you dirty Dad!

The boys came running in, piling in on him, thumping at ribcage, shoulders, head and shin—tugging, poking hard. Out of joyous rage that they had been deceived, that he had supplanted them at the forbidden set.

Dad, oh Dad, that's not fair.

Whoa, he said, settle down.

That settled nothing. They punched and pulled, yanked at his hair, joined in a death grip on his throat.

Say you're sorry, Dad.

I'm—

What are you saying, Dad?

—sorry, boys.

They climbed up him, snuggled in. Snuggled close. To touch something alive and warm. Do you remember, sons? This is the way a real person feels.

What's your favourite, Dad?

My favourite what? Program, woman, son?

Your favourite program, Dad. I know what mine is.

Where's your mother, boys?

38

Oh Dad, not that again!

Idiots-at-large, idiot image of Rose and him—and we are responsible for what they might become. If I was taken for ransom how much would they give to have me back? $4 from their piggy-bank if it interfered with no plans of theirs. In a reasonable age he would be thrown into chains, be dragged to jail, taken up and hanged. In a reasonable age. They stared a moment at the changing show. *Here Comes Lucy* was coming on fast—another can of worms.

I'm hungry, when's dinner, Dad?

I don't know.

What're we having, Dad?

Disappearing Mom.

Aw, Dad.

She wasn't coming home. Nell had wised up finally and gone away for good. I'm going to leave you, Talbert, one day you know I will.

Excuse me, sons.

He elbowed free, ran down the hall to the bedroom. She might leave but never without her $50 bottle of Joy. He approached her dressing table, sorted through vials, tubes, sachets and bottles. Here was chypre and jasmine and sandalwood, Replique and Aplomb and civet oil and her birth control pills—but none of her precious Joy.

She's gone, he told the boys. From here on out we're on our own.

Oh don't be silly, Dad, don't worry so fucking much.

Do I worry, Rose? Rose, am I worried now? He went to his closet, pulled out his lumberjack coat which smelled of smoke and fish, of grass and wood. Pulled on his box-top game warden's badge. Felt for his wallet, forgetting he had misplaced it somewhere.

Where are you going, Dad?

To find Nell, he said. Maybe she's out there on the road,

run down by a yellow Porsche with a girl on the hood. Maybe she's up there in the hills, run down by a rampaging moose. Out there in trouble, just waiting for me to appear. You guys behave, get your dinner, put on your pyjamas, you don't want to catch cold. Do your homework, go to bed, don't sweat it, I'll be back soon.

Don't worry about us, Dad.

He went outside, stood in the yard. It was dark now, a reversed smog bowl in soft romantic illumination above the city.

Where to begin?

Igor? Is it safe? They are not asleep.

Igor lifted the latch. Slid through. Here he was in control, no-one could instruct him. He was the master of these homes. She entered behind him, holding her breath. The house seemed hollow, ghost-occupied. The darkness in which she moved was alive, breathing—welcoming this intrusion.

Where are you, Igor? Igor, shouldn't we wait until they go to bed? I hear children, Igor.

Igor's hand closed over her mouth. You have to rush these houses, he said. You have to show them who is boss. His voice was so quick it snapped: Igor the housebreaker filling the skin of Igor the languid lover.

Igor, whose house is this? Igor, I can't see.

You have to feel it, he said—or go home.

She reached for him but he was gone. She stretched out her arms, felt about, could find nothing. It might have been a cave underground, a black box empty except for her. She moved. Nothing scraped, nothing toppled. Nothing fell. She moved with more purpose now, confident that in this utter blackness nothing would get in her way.

The house even feels familiar. I can do it, Igor. I find I have a talent for this.

Again Igor was beside her, this time a light touch on her

arm. His whisper matched her own: Yes, you're doing very well. Let's go. Let's see what kind of life we have here.

She clutched at his sleeve: I *know* this house, she whispered. It's amazing, Igor! I was made for this work! I can feel the life of this house pulsing in my blood! What do I do now?

Once more she was left alone. The house seemed to vibrate, waiting, a willing partner to this violation. In a hush now, she advanced. She would have to discover for herself that it wasn't the entering—but the leaving that was hard.

If You Love Me Meet
Me There

From a window in the room at the front of his house he looks out now across the high-strung weeds to their place. They have come for her. They are taking her away. Finally she is dead.

I had not expected this. I entered this room only because here I have a chair in which I like to sit and my work and my books and these two windows which hold me here.

One window faces the street, the other his driveway and the square pink house where the woman has lived and where at last she is dead.

I have seen only two people although I have been watching for some time. Of course the others are inside. The Rambler station wagon is parked in the yard. On the street shoulder are two other automobiles I have not seen before. Two men have been standing together near these; now they are moving toward the house. There is a hearse as well—it moves out of the driveway, turns left into the street. It passes my house and is gone.

A moving figure catches his attention—a tall, well-built boy, seventeen years old, dressed now in a white uniform.

Yes, Tom. A bakery worker. He crosses the street, uses my driveway as a shortcut, and takes the path through the field to the house of the dead woman. It is a point of sorrow to me

*that although the path is directly between my house and that
of the dead woman I have never used it. Except for my son,
no-one in my house ever has. Hello, Tom.*

Tom has thrown up a sluggish hand; he has smiled sadly
and shrugged his shoulders and moves now slowly along the
path to the pink houe, his hands deep in his pockets.

I should leave this room. It's terrible my watching this way.

Three times since he has been living here the woman has
been taken to the hospital. Each time they have said she would
not last the night. Each time she has returned.

*Perhaps at any rate she has got what she wanted: to die at
home in her own bed. Cancer, I believe that's what I have
heard. With her husband she operated a florist shop down-
town. I've driven by, seen her there. Arranging flowers, taking
orders on the phone. A grey, bony woman with haunted eyes.
Christ!*

Now the black hearse has returned. It could not have gone
far. Perhaps the driver wanted cigarettes. Another car also has
appeared. It curves in off the street, passes the Rambler, is
halted in the scrubby grass near the front door. The children
emerge. The daughter is perhaps eight years old, she holds her
older brother by the hand. There is one other child, no more
than five, but he does not appear. The curtained windows of
the hearse glare in the sun.

*What a hot, still day this is. It is sordid of us not to pay our
respects. But we hardly know them, that's true. She must have
been a fine woman. She and her husband worked hard, they
were often together. And the children are well behaved.*

The children are skinny and shy. In truth they belong to an
earlier time. The house belongs to no time at all. It sits pink
in the measureless field which itself extends to a drab stand of
stunted pine. Some two or three outhouses lean in the back
yard. On their outside wall by the front door is a large red
Coca-Cola clock which keeps good time. The husband raises

chickens in a small way.

The last time I spoke to him he mentioned two matters: his wife was in the hospital again, was not expected to last the night, and my son's dog had been killing his chickens. I was uncomfortable, could not look at him.

He is aware that the dog has been killing the man's chickens. He has seen a scattering of feathers near the back door stoop and twice has found the dog trotting along with a dead chicken in his jaws.

My wife says to me, "What does he expect? His chickens are all over the neighbourhood and how can a dog not be a dog?"

It is not the dog that concerns her, nor is it the chickens. She senses in the matter a veiled displeasure with her son and is quick to defend him against these unreasonable claims.

Your dog has been killing my chickens, the man from the pink house says, but it is not the fault of your dog. He's a good dog. It's that small hound-pup from across the street who starts it all. He gets your dog excited, the two of them begin chasing the chickens. Chickens are fast but they run short of breath. I'll get some birdshot, he says. A shot of that on their rumps and they won't bother the chickens no more.

Come see us, he says—and goes.

—Come see us. Although he and his wife have many times invited us over we've never found the time. She was pleasant, he is too, but somehow their Coca-Cola clock has frightened us off.

He has said to the man on such occasions: Thank you, we would love to come, maybe tomorrow. He has sought to reconcile his personal inadequacy with a desire to be decent, has put on a long face and called: If there is anything we can do, let us know.

The man pauses, answers back: It's all a matter of time, I reckon. Lord knows.

He is resigned to it, you see. He has accepted her death as he has had to bear with the death of his chickens. There is not much he can do.

Well, it's happened now. She's dead. I guess in a way he must feel relieved.

The boy, Tom, is crossing back through the field between the two houses. He throws up a tired hand, mouthes a word against the vacant air. Drops his shoulders and slouches on. In her yard at the pink house the young daughter is hugging herself, watching his progress through the tall tufts of grass gone to seed—spots the flight of two dipping birds and turns in absent study of them. She wears a grey, full-length dress, bunched at the waist, hanging slack on her arms, and someone has put a rose in her dark hair.

She looks old. Anemic. She looks small for her age but my wife says no, she's about average. My wife agrees she's not right somehow. One night last week I discovered her out front, staring at our house. At these windows here. For a long time she did not move. My wife saw her also, opened the door, inviting her in. She came timidly into the front room, clutching herself.

What is wrong, Teresa? his wife had asked. Can we help?

The girl seemed not to hear. Silent, she stared through the open door at the nursery room, at the cradle in which the baby slept.

She'll fall out, she said at last. The baby will fall out and bang her head.

Oh no, she's safe, his wife said. She's perfectly safe.

The girl's lips trembled, her eyes glanced past theirs.

He says I'll die too, she said. We all do. It's the Will of God.

Then she had begun backing toward the door.

If we had moved toward her she would have broken into a run. A false word and she might have screamed.

It's dark, his wife had said. Would you like my husband to

45

walk you home?

I love the dark, the girl had said. I can go anywhere.

A moment later they had seen her dark shape streaking across the field.

Now she stands in watch of that space where birds had been. Her father has come outside to lean against the Rambler station wagon in the yard. He speaks to her and she moves on out of sight beyond the far side of the house. The sun tints his face red; he appears ill-at-ease in his tight beige suit as he leans in solemn regard of the driver slouched low behind the wheel of the shining hearse. The lawn around him is much eroded, bare red patches of earth interrupting the dusty green. At the rear of the house the girl shows, dragging by the leg a mangled plastic doll.

Country to the core. Is this what I held against them? A comic pair. He toothless in his overalls, she with her stringy hair and sad skin, nodding with every word he spoke.

Come see us, hear!

So like each other, so well-suited that my wife could even seize upon this, use them in her arguments: you'll never change, we're not right for each other, we can never be with each other the way they are over there.

You want a pink house? A Coca-Cola clock by your door?

I want you to love me the way he loves her.

She's dying. Is that the way you want to live?

Looking for a place to rent they had arrived eventually at this house here. He liked the windows in the room to the front, liked the way one looked out over the street to the grove of trees fanning away there, the way this second one had a view of the wide field leading to the peculiar pink house which was itself backed by trees, and he saw already his desk in here and his books and the heavy leather chair.

We've got to paint it first, my wife said. I want white walls everywhere. Yes, I think it will do.

46

They were painting in a back room, absorbed in the task, the evening the neighbours called.

"Anybody home?" That's what they said, and came right in, shouting, "Anybody home?" as they stalked through empty rooms, finally to find us splattered by paint, applying white rollers to the walls.

You'll ruin them good clothes, the woman said.

You've got it looking good and clean, the man said, I'll say that.

They introduced themselves, asked us our names. They stayed a long time, while we stood, my wife and I, the paint dripping down our sleeves.

Well, look at us! exclaimed the woman. Them standing there ever so polite and not telling us to go home so they can get on with their painting.

They kept telling us they knew we would like it here. The neighbourhood was nice and quiet, it was far enough from town to let you hear yourself think.

Winter's hard though, it'll cost you a heap to heat this place. Anyway, that's what the other people said. They painted too before they moved in. Now, come to see us, hear!

We liked them. We gave assurances that once we were settled we'd drop in. For them to do the same anytime they wished.

It did not happen that way. Protocol required their visit to be returned and it never was. When the grass got too high his wife worried him until he went out to cut it. The man from the pink house drifted over, spoke of grass and the weather, of his chickens and the floral shop and the changing neighbourhood. At times his wife stood by, smiling and nodding her head—but they found excuses when invited in.

No, supper's about on, but you come see us, hear!

One year now we've been living here. Only lately, from our son, did we learn the woman was ill, that she might die at any time. My wife has many interests. She wanted to plant a flower garden, bought seeds at the store. He saw her clearing a plot, drove to his shop, returned with six potted plants which he presented to her.

The weather turned hot. One burning Saturday she dragged out the hose, watering the plants in the heat of the day. Of course they died. Driving by on the street one day the man noticed this, returned that evening with twelve plants more, which he set out himself.

What are neighbours for? he asked. But next time wait until the cool of the day.

Many days this year the woman has sequestered herself away in the pink house, alone while her husband saw to the shop. Three times this year she has been hospitalized.

I must cook something for them, my wife has said. Perhaps I can offer to look after the kids. But she has stood here at the window with me. We have not had even the courage to express our solicitude. And it's too late now. I can't just walk up to the door and say I'm sorry.

Over at the pink house now three men in dark suits stand by the front door, looking at the clock. Now and then one will dig his heel in the soil, another will stoop, plucking a blade of grass. The man in the hearse has tossed out another cigarette, is sitting up and looking back at the house. The two male children are out back leaning against a chicken coop door. They take drags on cigarette butts picked up from the yard. Spit, and say a word or two, and kick their heels in the dirt. The child, Teresa, has drifted down into the woods.

Thank God, at last!

Outside, his son's dog has moved off his haunches in the shade of the porch and galloped barking to the street. The white Volkswagen bulks into sight, his wife's knuckles white on the wheel. It sputters up the driveway, creeping to a stop. The dog's paws scratch at the door on the passenger side. His wife alights, wrestles with her packages, pauses a moment now to study and evaluate the situation next door. The son escapes from the car, gives chase to the yelping dog.

She comes in, a certain poise and talent for these things not yet disguised by her helpless show:

"My God, the stores were like Christmas, I couldn't even go to the toilet without being poked in the ribs."

"So long as you went," he says.

She laughs, leaning with her grocery bags as she transfers their weight to the table.

"There are more in the car."

"I can't go out now," he says, "can I get them later?"

She kicks off her black suede sandals, shakes hair from her face, arches her brow: "You can't go out now?"

"No. Later, I'll get them later."

Her mouth struggles with a smile which, however, is submerged as she reaches under her dress to remove her pants. She steps out of her briefs, flips them onto a counter somewhere, and advances—cooler now, freer—to unpack her goods. "As you please."

He goes back to his room, to his windows at the front of the house. His son and the dog are over in the yard at the pink house, in discreet observance of the activity there. A black casket is being removed from the house and the men are having some trouble with it. It leans just a bit; a man has turned his ankle and lost hold.

Stay back, son. Stay out of the way.

The dog sniffs about in the yard, looking from the men to the boy. He is no doubt baffled by this interruption in their play. The man in the beige suit trails after the casket, pausing now to ruffle the boy's head. For a moment the boy walks along with him, closely attentive as the men open the gate of the hearse and slide the cruel black box inside. He falls back as the hearse's engine turns, as the dead woman's husband gathers his children, heads them toward the Rambler in the yard. The hearse drags slowly up the street.

"When did she die?"

His wife sidles up to him, joins him at the window. She has changed out of her dress, is buttoning up her jeans, has her hair tied babushka-style by something that will presently serve as a curtain sash.

"I don't know. Do you think they'll be all right? The man and the children, I mean."

"If you knew they wouldn't, what would you do?"

She is not interested in any answer he would have to this. She quits the room, is next seen approaching the car.

She's right about me. I can't so much as bring the groceries in. But I had to watch the baby, there's that. I couldn't just wrap the baby up and take her over there.

The hearse moves somberly by the house. Behind it the Rambler comes, the boy Tom at the wheel. The little girl sits up front and the man and his two sons sit erect in the rear.

There they go.

Fearful of being seen, he steps back from the window, missing the tentative wave of the man inside the car. In a little while it will be dinner time.

The poor woman, he will say, cancer is such a terrible affair.

She didn't die from cancer, his son will say. Esther had leukemia as everyone knows.

Memoirs of a Cross-Country Man

Though the days are heavy, the nights they are starry-eyed. The first night at Estalavita Monastery I have terrible dreams which none of whom come true fortunate to say. In the dream I am like the beast being stroked after the long and fearful journey over hills, sweat guzzling off the hide and the hair slicked down, smooth hand on the rump and the sugar cube in the mouth, a cool voice whispering in the deadness of the ear: "A mangy jackass, him, too bad he have to carry such a heavy load." The voice in the ear is the talking in my head, the ear opposite asking what was said. And the talk goes on. Each minute of the darkness of the night I wake myself leaping from the bed, crying *Where am I?* Crying next *Marguerite, where are you?* Stumbling in the dark to close my arms on air. Falling back inside the rippling dream to say *Ahh, here she is!* To drift along under the soft waterfall of her touch along the thighs.

In sleep González is as much awake as he will ever be. And though the days are heavy, the nights they are starry-eyed. I go about Estalavita like a man entombed: working, walking, gnawing on the thumb. As much walking on my head as I am on the feet, half the time not knowing where I am while the prison of the body and the poison of the well and the sweet harmony of the torpedo acid tubes meet to decide which will make the final claim. Mouth hanging open, the bowels too weak to turn, myself too blind to tell the difference if they do. Our first day at the Pasadoke Hotel Marguerite have said to the fat grinning man behind the desk, "Where is a good place to get something to eat and drink?" And reach for the comic book to ask again *Dónda está un lugar bueno para ir a comer y tomar algo...* and that question now tumble over in my head to make me sick, the thought of drink, of food, the thought of Marguerite. Flushed face and changing smile, oh perfect picture then the happy bride! Now a loss that sickens too. And in the sky a puff of plane exploding the face of my poor mother everywhere.

"Busy yourself," the good Brother John advise.

I do, I do. I scrub out the pots and pan, plant food in the garden outside the wall, hoe and rake and sweep the trash, scrub down the cell and wash the back of the good Brother John and before the door the apple peel of the bad Brother Sam and look out the way for the lost crazy man who wander in one day looking he say for the search of the holy Grail. Oh, there are all sorts here and I make myself useful to this bunch you bet, never mind the bull, never mind the banging of the head on the stones of the wall, the mutterings of the head in the sleeve, the trampling of the feet on nails. . . never mind, I say to myself, for González Manuel he is not so far gone he don't know a good deal when he see.

"Maybe," I say to Brother John, "maybe I stay on, turn the spade here, wear me a gown, go barefoot on the soil, grow old and die unbeknown to the loved ones far away who never give a thought to me, I help you all for all my life González is a hard-working mule. González have found his place in the world, never mind this place be a tomb and I blow away to dust if ever I come again to fresh air."

"You got it bad," John say, "but I think you'll live."

That much they say and more, these crazy men, and even old Brother Sam, sorry as bastard ever was born, always kick you when you scrubbing the wall, punch your nose and starve you naked for the kindest word, even he will have to say in the end *Favour him O Father the poor miserable halfbreed, the poor mangy wop González Manuel, for in my heart I believe he has atoned for his evil and cannot help his stupid ways.*

I look it, that much to be sure, the mangy lowdown wop who steal the hubcaps even while the car is moved, who yank from the mouth the last biscuit of the starving Pariah dog, but who can help what he look who have been through where I have gone? I smack the first bastard say it isn't true and maybe I smack you just because!

In the meantime I work along with the ways of the time at hand. González Manuel he a man of many moods, be something in this world his moods if they last more than the second quick. Even in the dreams sometime I am a burden for the mushness of the heart, crying up forgiveness for the sorry son-ofbitch who poison me at the well, for Marguerite who leave me flat, even for the man in the street I never see. . . for all the bastardmen who hit me everywhich time I turn and kick me in the teeth when I am begging please—even him I forgive for a man can afford if he know that somewhere once in the world is a woman like Marguerite who have give her love to him and maybe no doubt would send her best if even now she know where to send.

O shit in no time at all I am a man again. The first day after the sleep I have already become Christian in the concept of the holy brothers of the monstery. A private ceremony with Brother John who baptize me from the heathen way and confess my sins, saying *Now repeat after me:*

I know Father I have sinned because the heart is a bare and naked bone.

I know Father I am unworthy for my head is like unto a

cloud of dust.

Sure, a drunkard he can spit on stone but González Manuel on the safe side will make no fool of God. A man come up slow when he fall where I have been: he come up with a slow look around and a sharp eye to the blind spots everywhere. Smart you bet, never no more the hatrack where the head should be. To the blind spot come the chop that take the head with it to the frying pan. If not the blind side then look out straight ahead. It is the man looking you straight in the eye pretty as you please, saying *What a nice day, González, how-deedoo, I be glad to help you any way I can, food, drink of water from the well, whatever you could want for I am here to serve*—oh you look out for him, I tell you this, for just when you saying to yourself *This one good Joe sure as the day I'm born, just the best sonofbitch I ever see*—why just then the bastard will haul out the axe and send your head flying half-way up the mountain top.

It take a time but I have learn: never look a man in the eye. Look at the sky, look at the shoe, stand awhile and shuffle the feet, and when you ready to go, back up and take the long way round. Once you stare the bastard in the eye he good as have you in the eye of the fucking storm.

"I know what you mean," say Brother John. "I been that road myself."

"A man of my nature," I say to him, "how he to live his days? Dusting the britches of whoever hand him the broom? Shit, now what you say to that?"

The bastard smile and wave his hand: "Some men are born," he say, "to wave the wand, others to record the magic fact, most to slave till the magic comes, to push the dirt and hoard up strength against that time when the dirt pushes them."

He carve the bread and grin, easy to see González Manuel is all of him ears. "You want me to tell you," he say, "what your life has been, to tell you what death is? God knows, if all

54

the black holes of the earth were placed one inside the other and then you were placed inside the smallest, the blackest of these, then that would be your life up to now. What travels you've had, González, they've all been on the wings of a darkness formed by all the lives you've left behind. Leaving life and entering death in your present state, you'd never know you'd made a turn. The final loneliness distinguishes the living from the dead and I ask you, one poor motherfucker asking another, where do you think you are now? You're like me, you don't know. Who the hell does? The body does not immediately yield up all its parts, neither expect the spirit to enter into all of hers. Have you entered the room of a dying man? That's what the hush is all about. The crazy doctors can't fix a proper time of death because they can't measure the spirit pull. All those fucking ghostly Helens mucking up the air! Shit, González, man is illness personified, how can he know when he will die? Your life, you turd, has been one long attempt to come to grips with your own passing from this passing world, you've wanted it to be simple as signing your X to the dotted line. Put down the X, you've said, and let the grave be filled. That's why you've invented this stupid goddamn story about some bastard at a well trying to poison you!"

Invent! When I am passed out with fever by the well and seventeen days delirious through the screaming sand, falling on my face a thousand times before I face up to falling here? Invent! With the bastard spic buzzards crawling on the head one day and the clothes all gone where the sorry man at the well have stolen even them! Naked through the desert crawling every mile! "Shit," I say, "maybe you tell me where the invention end?"

John, he carve off the cheese and drink the wine and lean back to study me. "Oh, nonsense," he finally say, "González, I saw you with my own eyes: you crawled into these walls like a man crawling out of a thousand caves. The truth is you like

55

and demand your lowly state, you've got a craving to be the downtrodden man. I submit—goddam, with all earnestness I do—I submit that the days you lay stinking at the well, the days you crawled sick, hungry and burning across those baking hot miles to this place represented your closest communion with man. If you're honest I believe you'll admit that those experiences were the most satisfying you've ever known, more satisfying by far than this wretched love of Marguerite you talk so much about. You shit, you recognized the spirit pull! You hit for that stage of painlessness beyond the pain! While with Marguerite, if my guess is right, you recognized what life could be with all your dark boxes gone, with sunlight on your brow. And being the crazy fucker that you are, you recoiled. You couldn't even consummate your wedding vows."

How he know? The bastard monks they look you in the eye and root the sorry secret out. And now he have that much still he root some more. He stab the knife in the carving board, put down the cheese, and study my face hard.

"I've been wanting to ask you," he say, "about all this wop business you talk about. Your blue eyes interest me. For instance I've been wondering, goddamn you, how they got that way. In my experience two figs do not make a peach. But we can go into that another time, I guess: what puzzles me now is why you talk the way you do—that absurd pidgin-English you fill your mouth with. In your sleep—hell, in those crazy dreams of yours!—I've seen you talking straight as I'm talking now. Is it because you see yourself a fool? You refuse to present yourself seriously for fear that seriously you've nothing to present? Is that it?"

What I say? Once in the city by the river when I am with Marguerite she say that very thing to me. You don't fool me, she say, not one little bit. What I *can* say except a man his own lifestyle is all he have. He have more I have *her* with me now. When a man lose the style he go looking for the flair. That gone, then he can go looking for the dotted line, for Mr. X to hold his hand. Shit, seven years I been to night school, three years I go to Harvard-Yale, shit I am in good standing with the American Academy of the Poets and read every word of the encyclopedia job I sell, not to mention the money I spend to buy the taco stand. All the same a man who never know where he get off neither do he know where he get on. At the wedding in the church Marguerite introduce me saying, "González, you remember Miss Hannah, I'm sure," and who is it in front of me but a woman I never seen before who smile and say, "O yes! you're that nice orderly who left Margy the flower in the jar when she was sick!" and to myself I say, "Me? Where?" Later she take me aside, say, "Psssst, let's share secrets, let's," and she say sure she remember me good, good to see me again now, got one good girl I have, be good to Margy and take care —but listen, she say, never breathe a word to her that I was the one left the flower in the jar, I stole it from that awful grouch Gladys Beer, the lady with the boils, sure you remember her, Jesus what a case!

And then she trip off to leave González tripping on himself, which way knowing where to turn? What hospital? When? I never see you before, Miss Hannah, never see Marguerite as a child sick. One time I work the hospital sure but I am down in the basement blackface shoveling coal to the boiler room, keeping close watch the gauge which the bossman say will blow the whole shebang skyhigh one day. Sure, and never see these people seeing me, leaving flowers in the jar, never setting eyes on Marguerite you bet, otherwise I marry her long before.

Who is González Manuel is why he talk the way he do but *who is he* is the question yet. God knows a man on the run, a man who leave running every place he go, he not have time to sit back with blowing smoke from the pipe, careful polish of the phrase or spit shine on the shoe! Who you know can speak like the prince when inside he know he is being made the

57

clown?

"You can lead the burro to the water hole," I tell that man John, "but how can he be made to shout *Olé*?"

"If you are a man who has been led there," he say, "if you are not a mule then the *Olé* is every place you look. It's the looking that brings it there. Take my case now: my mother, as sorry a little waterhole as ever you saw—my mother took in strangers for the night. 'Straight blow or round-the-world?' That's what she'd say to them: you think that wasn't hard on me? And Father. Father killed a man in Richmond, Indiana, another in Bull City, Arkansas, a third in Montreal, Quebec. These are all they traced. Mother spent her best years trying to get me sent to him, saying a boy needed a dad and didn't I need him? I arrived with my bags and a note from her to him in Sacramento, California on the day he was being gassed! He'd been caught finally but the case was one of mistaken identity. A friend had used his name while successfully murdering three in a family of four. The fourth insisted my father was the man who had sliced the throats of her parents and her brother, aged ten. The same friend who had accomplished this told me so himself, he bought me coffee and pie and admitted he would kill me too if I breathed a word. The surviving girl in the murdered family fell in love with me and I with her, we were to be married but at two o'clock in the morning on the day the wedding was to take place a TWA jetliner crashed into the house of the uncle and aunt with whom she was staying, killing 78 persons on board, not to mention the aunt and uncle and the girl herself. This friend of my father found me in the city of Miami, demanded money from me not because he felt I owed it to him but because he simply was down on his luck and didn't know who next to kill. I pitched him out the window of the ninth floor room of the Sheraton-Plaza hotel but what the police didn't know was that he was dead before he hit the street. True, I swear to God! He'd had a heart attack when he realized through me that death was staring him in the face. A fire in the hotel that night killed another 36 and I was a hero, single-handedly saving four people from Idaho trapped in their rooms. A happy story? Listen, my mother shot herself in desperation one evening when one of the strangers wanted to drink rum when all she had was gin. He had dared her to shoot as an example that she cared. I held her head in a towel while he phoned for the ambulance and fled. That same night in a period of two hours nine women were raped at knife-point within a mile of where we then lived. Upwards of a hundred people witnessed these acts but none stepped forward to halt them and not one witness agreed as to what the rapist wore. Need I tell you that man was me? Soon afterward I placed myself as novice here. And my past is beautiful compared with the past of most of my brothers here. Now I write psychoanalytic articles for the learned journals and use the small payment to support the works of poverty, celibacy, obedience to our superior grace, and love. Otherwise I pray. I find you refreshing to talk to, González, for you strike me as one vastly unlike myself: you're a victim as I was but, unlike myself, it isn't because you've acquired the taint of sin. You can't tell me about your well because I know the goddam place better than you ever will."

He stands, taps finger to brow, scrapes crumbs from the jaws: "A lovely meal. Now come along with me. It's time you met our chief, Father-Padre, who is double father to all the brothers here. Come. Come."

A man can bleed from the heart, knowing soon it will bleed no more. There come a time when he is willing to kiss the foot of the man who wipe the shoes on the head. If I feel bad then I don't know yet González is a lucky man. The night I make the visit to the Father-Padre is the same night a sane man flees. The Father occupy the cell at the end a narrow hall, dark and cold, up high somewhere in the monastery wall. Up high too a single window which hove in the sun on shiny days, thin beam of light over the bare stone wall, across the bare stone floor, and the very air it is damp, bare and cold. Father-Padre himself resemble no man González Manuel have ever seen, bleak features in the clouded face which afterward I cannot recall to say this is how the Father looked or even this was how he seem. Tall figure in the white robe, bare red toes upon the stone, he does not walk he flows, wisp of dank musty odour moving in the faint darkness of the cell. Down across the brow and winding down past the cheek a wide purple scar looking fat upon the sunken skin, the thinnest man in all the world and tall enough to stoop for doors. Sometime somewhere someone have pull all the nails from the fingers, all the hair from the head and the skin have the colour purple like a man who have come back from the grave if ever he have got that far without falling down, in his eyes are the calm depths of a man who never dream.

It is cold enough to freeze the nuts between the legs.

You feel unloved, González Manuel? Estalavita loves you. You have been ill-used? We will not ill-use you here. God is nothing, man is less. Are you hungry? In the kitchen there is soup, porridge, bread and cheese. I myself partake only of bread, a raw egg once each day. What we have is yours, what you have is ours. As you have come many have come before. As you leave so will others go. We are one with you, you are one with us.

Father-Padre he does not speak with words, at the end of the cell a writing stand which have a camera set behind. Built into the opposite wall and to the walls of other cells where I work I have found the green face of the television screen which take closed circuit his message every wall. The message unroll on the screen like a man turning the wheel by the hand.

You will have observed I have no crucifix on the wall, no chain around my neck. Who is God if not me—and you? The soul serves, as does the floor for my feet without the need of shoes. Assume I know your thoughts, your trials: each place you have been I have been before. In this cell for seven years I have stood: it is forbidden that I take rest by sitting or lying down. Once each month for one hour I am transported into the courtyard for sun and it has been noticed that where I tread, the grass nevermore will grow. All around us are dying men, the best of these I attempt to summon here as I have summoned you. Call upon me when you wish, make no regard for light or day. If I am here, but gone in a manner you shall understand, do not be afraid. Stay for what length you must, share in what comforts you may find: we are an extension of yourself. In what other way can your happiness exist? We of this order are bound by rule and practice the councils of perfection as best we can. There is no finish, there is no end and while there is corruption anywhere there can be no perfect man and for this reason Estalavita has latitudes of grace. Our most exacting rule is our confinement to these walls since in our imperfection we can hurt no-one but ourselves. Howevermany light years we remove ourselves from the common laws of man these laws remain no less embedded than is manhood itself embedded within the rock and clay and our mixtures within the clouds. I do not mean to be obtuse. My whole attention rests not on you nor even on the difficulties which brought you here. No man may leave running but something of value is left behind. History is the truth of this and in the running the place we have run to is not better nor worse than that place behind. God is wicked, man is no less. We have passed from darkness into light and into darkness again and with each passing the shadows have not changed. And death makes no room for you. Leave nothing behind when you go. Arriving, nothing will have been there before. You are one with me, I am one with you. Sisters in light are brothers in darkness before. The eye of the storm is brainless, it occupies a centre and is powerful beyond reckoning, it goes where it goes.

The screen is blank now, nothing on it shows. The drum rolls empty inside the screen as the idea flowing outside my head. I am at peace I think but who can call me satisfied? Despite all the good intention of Father-Padre, González is no nearer to where he was. Face to the spangled boughs of desert scrubs the crooked sky is fading under the cold flush of the rising moon. At his point in the corner the Father stands silent, not one eye move or muscle shift, he is nothing short of dead. Outside the window a flutter of wings, in the sky a black bird flying for the trees.

And in the corridors of the hall there is the smell of water sweating on the stone, the musky damp of moss around a tomb. I don't know why I think of death but it is what González feel. My own footsteps slide along the wall and come back to me echoes like the walk of someone dead. A man in my state is in no hurry to go fast, no haste to move at all. Black space is at my rear, even blacker is the space before. If I am not dead myself then González have the sense of the dead following slow behind. It remind me of the time I am a child alone in the room, alone in the black house waiting for the mother to come, for the day to come when the ghosts are gone. A man can stop where he is and stare all the way through the black dark to the childhood days to see himself trembling as he tremble then and if he is honest he can admit to himself González the childhood have followed you each step the way or even plead inside the heart sonofbitch don't follow me no more.

Housed in the vaults along the corridor walls the dead brothers of the sect. One above the other for all the distance the candle goes. Living with the living is not enough now I have also I think to live with the dead. And all the time I am wanting to run a long shriek is climbing inside the throat and a busy hand pushing from the rear. For I know something else to come, one more vault to find, my own. *González*, the deathman say—*are you there?* One time maybe I was—but now? In the dark the truth and the lie sleep side by side, face to face: one day when the dark is black enough maybe the lie will turn and run. *González, are you there?* Only Marguerite knows I am. I tell myself now that if she say I have left the flower in the jar and reveal it dry between the pages of the book who then knows better? She or me? Sure the darkness the answer knows but will it tell me?

Oh, the night is a busy one I have. Later on the crazy monk who search for the holy Grail come awake to say, "Got you now!" The eyelids roll, a second later he is dead. His body it is prepared for the vault within the walls, before the light of morning come it is sealed away behind the stone which read:

All-arm'd I ride, whate'er betide,
Until I find the holy Grail.

If he found it, the brothers say, let it go with him.

"Shit," Brother John say, "it takes a crazy man not to know he's had it all the time. The blood of God is never spilled, ours you'll find every day."

Sure and I come to find the thing in the bed I have been sleeping with is none other than myself. Myself that feels the shape I hold, the shape that will conduct the body over the wall of stones to the level digging earth which say finally HERE HE LIES. The truth is that the trouble with González have finally brought him low. Meanwhile the God who gives life to the biggest fool will say Carry on. When the last trumpet sound still will there be music in the ears. . . if not that then a clanging in the head. A natural death, the deathman say, is all the law allows. Shit the dream is in the sleep but what is in the dream? Sometime between the taking of the porridge and the chewing of the bread I find myself González back at the bridal rooms of the Pasadoke sending off to the newspaper the classified *ATTENTION READERS OF THE NEWS: When last seen she have blue eyes, about my height, wearing tight-fit English tweed high above the knees. Pantyhose neptune blue, no hat and alligator shoes. Reward offered, write me here, you be glad you did.*

Call Me Belladonna

The snow was coming down heavy so I ducked in for shelter at the first available door, and there she was standing by a rack of day-old glazed doughnuts as if she had been waiting for me.

"I'm worried," she said, before I could even say hello or brush the snow out of my eyes. The snow was melting against my neck and my fingers felt frostbitten because of the absurd gloves manufacturers make for women and the absurd length to which we will go in sustaining the slender image.

"About what?" I asked.

"About Tom."

She had my attention then. For a brief while earlier I had been close to Tom and there had been in Tom's mind at least some question as to which of us he would attach himself to. I looked at the doughnuts which were being sold three for a quarter and contemplated buying a few.

"What's the matter with Tom?" I asked.

"He mopes," she said. "He sulks. He's become a goddamn bore." She said a lot of other stuff too but I missed most of it because another person came in and was trying to get by, shaking his huge black coat and flinging snow all over us.

"Excuse me," he said, and I stepped irritably out of his way, as did Rebecca, who hadn't taken her eyes off me.

"That's too bad," I told her. "Sorry to hear it." I was surprised to discover that she'd lost a lot of weight, in the face actually, and more than seemed good for her. "Poor Tom," I said, "what can be the matter with him?" She grinned ever so slightly. I brushed past her, walking up to the bakery counter where I scratched on the stainless steel lid with my keys to get the attention of the sullen girl working there.

"Nice to see you," Rebecca said behind me, and I turned, nodding politely, perhaps murmuring something of the same. Her new face looked fatigued, she looked worn out and not at all happy. I had never liked her and felt no concern one way or the other.

She ducked her head down into her brown fur collar and charged out into the swirling snow.

Eventually I grabbed a taxi and managed to get home.

That day turned out to be the start of a big blizzard. For five days it snowed and no-one went anywhere. In the street fronting my apartment, cars were abandoned, strung out, whipped about like so many gentle white wrinkles, and during that time and for some days later, I remained inside nursing a cold and rather delighted to have it that way.

It was three weeks later that I chanced to see Tom. I say *chanced* though that's really not likely. I ran into him at the laundromat where under ordinary circumstances I go every Thursday. I came in with four queen-sized pillow cases filled with my dirty things and my mason jar filled with detergent. He was seated in a mold-poured plastic chair, his face hidden behind a three-month old copy of *Time*. That was unlike Tom whose only reading during the time I had known him was when he'd check over the TV schedule or look over my shoulder at a cookbook to learn what he was having for dinner and whether he could bear to eat it. He hadn't shaved in several days, I noticed, but that's the filthy kind of habit not uncharacteristic of him. He didn't look up so I went on through the

66

elongated ugly room hunting for enough washers side by side and near the dryers too.

I had already realized the washing was going to take up all of my evening.

I had figured too that I would be bound to run into the prick sooner or later.

My sheets alone filled two of the machines and I was sliding my money in the coin slots on a third when I felt his hand touch my shoulder from behind.

"You've been out of town," he said.

"No. No," I told him. I didn't look at him.

"Sure you have," he said. "I tried ringing you."

"No," I said. "No, you didn't."

"Once or twice," he said. "Honest. Where did you go? I wish I could get out of the city. I never go anywhere. I haven't been out of this city since I was a kid."

I poured in the soap and banged the three lids down and walked down the long aisle searching for two more Speed Queens side by side.

"I guess you went out to the island," he said, tagging along behind me. "Did you see Phil? How is Phil and the family?" he asked.

I told him I hadn't seen Phil in ages. I told him I hadn't been anywhere, that I had been down with the flu.

He said he had had it too.

The cycle had finished on machines 18 and 19 and I removed someone's wet laundry, jamming it into two red plastic baskets the management keeps around for that purpose. Then I loaded the empties with the rest of my dingy stuff, one for the whites and the second for the coloureds. I put in the money and got the cycles going and then carried the first of the red baskets over to the table. I asked him if he'd bring the other one over but he had on his dreamy look and paid no attention. I brought that one over and placed it beside the first and poked

67

at the stuff on the top because it seemed to me their owner had overloaded and I doubted whether the wash was clean.

Then I went back to check on my first three machines. I was thinking how long it had been since I had needed five machines or come in with four pillow cases full.

He was standing by the door looking outside, not at all erect, his eyes a little glazed, looking weary. When he moved out we had spent two hours getting all his stuff together. Just when I thought I had it all collected and ready for the walk down to the laundromat I had come across three or four months of dirty socks and underwear and smelly shirts thrown loosely away in the back of his closet. The air fresheners are still hanging there now because the empty closet still carries his stench.

"Where were you last Thursday?" he asked.

I didn't say anything.

I was finished now with the machines, had nothing to do until their cycle was completed, so I walked over to the bench and sat down. I had brought along a sandwich and an old issue of a magazine called *Furioso* that I'd found few months back in a used-book store. It had a poem in it that had attracted me, called "Signals From the Love Parlour" and I had brought it along because I'd not taken the time or trouble to read much more than the opening lines and tonight I had thought I might.

"What are you reading?" he asked.

"Nothing," I said.

He shrugged and scraped a chair over.

He stared at me for about two minutes. I kept waiting for him to ask me what kind of sandwich I was eating and it irritated me that he didn't. He finally picked up the *Time* he'd been reading earlier, and drowsed over its pages until I finished the sandwich and opened my own magazine again. Then he waved his flimsy crumpled *Time* absent-mindedly in the air and poked it toward me.

"It says here," he said, "that Nixon still feels he's going to beat it."

"Beat what?" I asked. "Death?" I really didn't know what he was talking about and for a moment actually experienced some mild curiosity and was reminded in a minute, brief way of the first time I had ever met him, one evening at a party when I had overheard him talking about an elderly woman's bleached hair.

"Yeah," he said. "it says here that Mitchell and Dean and one or two guys will get stuck with it. What do you think?"

He rolled the magazine up and sighted through it at me. Leaned there with his elbow resting on one knee, his head cocked to the side, running one hand through his hair while his lips curled back in a grimace and he bit down on his tongue.

"Watergate," he said. "You believe all this stuff?"

"Why don't you shave?" I asked.

"Don't have the time," he said. "Anyway, I'm not going anywhere."

He threw the magazine back on the table. "I figure he's right," he said. "Nixon didn't get where he is by being stupid. I figure he must know what he's talking about."

I closed the magazine on my finger and looked up at the pink concrete walls, holding my gaze there, thinking that if I stared long enough at a single spot, that spot would be reamed and the hole would enlarge and take the rest of the pink wall away with it, take Tom and the Speed Queens and all the imprisoned filth and disagreeable odours, and that when the hole filled again and the wall came back someone else would be sitting where I was sitting for I would be off somewhere asleep in fine clover and Tom would be packed away in a scented, inexpensive coffin. Here it was 1973, Christmas coming on, the snow all gone, and Tom still in his cheap loose clothing with his four days' growth of beard, looking out at me with his dull eyes that still didn't know, and wouldn't care if he did know, that Nixon was an established son of a bitch and that he, Tom, was one more pathetic blotch in a long caravan.

"What's the matter?" he asked.

I could forgive myself for the vicious ones, for the self-esteemed ones; I could even tolerate the square-jawed, round-eyed "we-are-dominant" ones and the "all-women-are-tramps" ones, but how could I vindicate myself for association with those like Tom?

"What's the matter?"

I shook my head and went back to the contents page to try to find the stupid poem I'd lost again.

"You don't agree?" Tom said. "You think he's guilty?"

I got up to check out the machines, thinking maybe I had put too much soap in them since that's what I usually do. I do it and the soap flows out the top, it keeps on bubbling over until it has run out across the sidewalk and into the gutter and every time I glance up at the big sign on the wall reading:

PLEASE DO NOT PUT IN EXCESS SOAP
AS THIS CAUSES DAMAGE TO THE MACHINES
AND GIVES A POOR WASH LIKEWISE.

I get nervous such times and examine every person who comes in, worried that one of them will be the owner or the manager or perhaps some tight-lipped customer who will start cursing and complaining and will want to throw me out into the street and my clothes out on top of me washload after washload. The owner goes crazy over slugs or bent coins or too much soap but if the machines break down midway through the cycle, six attorneys couldn't pry your 35 cents out of him.

This time I had put a little too much in two of them, the soap was beginning to bubble up out of the lid, though I didn't think there would be much trouble.

Tom shoved my chair out toward me with his foot when I came back.

"Thanks," I said, and he tried to grin nicely. I found myself staring at his nails. They hadn't been cut in a long time, which didn't surprise me, though I was puzzled by one curious feature: the nails on his right hand were really quite remarkably clean while those on his left had thick black crusts under them.

"You ever think," he said, "how expensive this gets?"

It was his conversational tone and I shook my head, opening my review again, fanning the pages for "Signals From the Love Parlour."

"I mean," he said, "35 cents each, you got five machines, that's how much?—$1.75? Then you probably got 50/60 cents worth of soap, more than that if you buy those little ounce packages out of the vending machine. So $2.25, say, and then another dollar on top for the dryer. You'll have to have two dryers at a minimum, I'd guess."

He paused. I thought he was through but he wasn't.

"In a year's time," he said, "that could amount to $100 or so, not to mention the cost to a person in time when he sits around here waiting for the job to get done. My point is you could probably look in the want ads and buy your own washer for close to $50."

I closed my eyes a minute and breathed deep. Blowing now and then the way they tell you to do at the Lamaze class, which I count as the only practical advice I've ever received. Then I got out a cigarette and lit up. I waited for him to ask for one but he simply looked sullenly on and said nothing. The ammonia/detergent smell was getting to me so I walked out on the sidewalk and stayed there smoking, pulling the smoke deep down in my lungs, staring at the cars passing and at the staggered lights in the high buildings all around, trying to decide whether any recognizable pattern was to be detected in the mixture of darkness and light. I stamped the cigarette out after

71

an inch or so had burned down, and turned back inside because the machines were clattering and humming and mine would be shifting into its rinse cycle. Tom had his chair tilted back against the wall, hands behind his head, his legs stretched out.

"Becky ran into you, I understand," he said.

"Rebecca did," I said. I opened my journal again.

"She mentioned it," he said. "Back there during the snow. During the blizzard. Said she ran into you."

I detest such speech rhythms. Maybe one day it will drive me to poetry too and one will find me writing lines like

Shadow master,
do vulture wings disguise
your jewels,
when you cradle the dreaming dark
do trash cans contain your thunder?

—though I hope not.

"She said you looked nice."

I nodded.

"She said you looked pretty terrific, actually."

"That was nice of her," I said.

He blinked a few times in satisfaction, as if to say that took care of that. I looked away at a man who had walked in carrying a wicker laundry basket, a lovely boy of four or five walking along at his side, dressed in a denim coat and trousers. The boy was licking on a candy bar that was dripping chocolate over his hand. I stared at him, at the boy and at his hand, thinking how strange it is that small children's hands really do get so hot and sweaty, that their small bodies really do seem to burn when they sleep, that they pick up something and it quickly melts in their hands and they get filthy all over and everyone bitches at them, forgetting that it isn't the child's fault for how is the child to know that his hands have such a peculiar characteristic?

He had exceptionally fair skin and beautiful blond hair cut in a page-boy style.

The father was tall, with a solemn demeanour, and he was irritably lifting the boy up so he could peer into one of the machines.

"Are those our clothes too?" the boy asked, and the man shook his head, placing him back on the floor and walking down the rank of washers looking for one that was empty. He lifted lid after lid and when he arrived at the last and lifted it he turned and looked over at us in a questioning, half-baffled manner. He was dressed in a nice tan suit ever so casually rumpled, and wore a blue dress-shirt with a fringe and open at the neck. He had the same blue eyes as his kid who had quit banging on the dryer window to go stomp in the soap puddle in front of my machines.

His father told him to behave.

I got up to check on nos. 18 and 19, and mentioned to the father that he should select a machine that had completed its cycle and place the contents into one of the red plastic baskets.

He drew nearer, politely smiling, speaking with a persuasive gentleness that would have nauseated me when I was younger.

"Is that the practice? No-one will object?"

The kid left the puddle to come up and see what kind of person his father was talking to, though when he reached his father he barely glanced at me. He was more interested in Tom. Tom had rolled up my magazine and was slapping it against his open palm.

"Don't do that, please," I told him.

He gave me an odd glance and, shrugging, put it aside.

"I'm four," the boy said, and slowly, as if he had arthritis in his fingers, peeled off the numbers. The father said something to him, and both drifted away.

Tom came up and touched my elbow.

"She said you were crying," he said.

My head snapped around. I was surprised and angered and told him that was a damn lie. "Why would I have been crying?" I asked. "She must be crazy!"

"No," he said, "I mean she said she thought at first you were crying and then she saw it was only because of the cold or something like that or because some snowflakes got caught in your eyelids and melted when you got inside the store and so she thought you were crying."

"Well," I said, "I wasn't."

"She did say you looked good," he said. "She said you were walking with a real spring in your step and not taking any shit off anyone. I told her she probably had you confused with someone else." He laughed as he said the last but when I didn't smile he soon stopped.

"How did you think she looked?" he asked.

"Tired," I said. "Pretty. A little restrained."

"That's what I think," he said. "She takes everything too seriously."

We watched the man empty no. 12. The boy asked if he could put their clothes in and his father told him to go ahead.

"What did she tell you about me?" Tom asked.

His voice had changed on the question and I regarded him soberly, smiling despite myself. His face had gone quite serious. I noticed thin white streaks around the mouth, beneath the splotchy black beard, and there were lines around his eyes that I didn't remember.

"Did she mention me?" he repeated. "What did she say? I know she told you something."

The small boy had come up to look us over. He had been dropping articles of clothing on the dirty floor and his father had ordered him away. He stood facing us, his hands busy, simultaneously picking at his nose and fingering his penis because he had to go to the bathroom.

74

"She didn't say much," I told Tom. "We were together only a few seconds."

"You're kidding," he said. "She told me you two talked for half an hour."

I didn't argue with him. The boy had moved up to within a foot of Tom, interested apparently in his beard but at the same time holding his penis and dancing up and down, his face contorted. The boy's father was fumbling through his pockets for change, murmuring to himself. He crossed over to the dispensing machine, dropped in a dime, and pulled the lever for the detergent nearest him, one called Target. The boy went running over, yelling that he wanted to do it and asking what that was.

I lit up another cigarette and walked out onto the sidewalk. The air was fresh and cool, it smelled damp and pleasant after inhaling the bleach odour inside. Tom followed me out and stood nearby, his head down, humming a tune of no particular distinction or description, which is the way he usually gets when he has something on his mind.

"We didn't talk long," I told him. "I came in to get out of the snow and cold and saw Rebecca there. I may have said hello, or she may have, though I don't think so."

"What did you think of her new hair style?" he asked.

I told him we had been bundled up in heavy coats, had been wearing kerchiefs and hoods and I hadn't much noticed.

"She changed it about a month ago," he said. "Got it cut short. Looks idiotic, if you ask me. What else did she say? About me, I mean."

"She told me she was worried about you. I think that's all she said."

"That's all?"

"Then she left."

"Oh come on," he said, "she must have said more!" He had his hand around my wrist and was trying to pull me around in front of him. I don't know why men feel they have to yank and twist a woman around like that. I don't know why if he wanted to look at my face he couldn't have walked the few steps around me to get the view he desired. But men are like that. I know that some women are too but we never are in quite the same way. I have pulled men around like that, or tried to when I was angry or disgusted with them or when I was distressed and a wreck inside and wanting some attention given to me—but I don't do it indiscriminately and I can't hurt them anyway.

"Let go of my wrist," I told him.

He let go immediately. He cocked his head to the side, looking off above me, kicking one heel against the pavement and ramming his hands into his pockets.

I studied him for a moment, inhaling the cigarette, letting the smoke stream out through my nostrils the way I used to do when I first learned how. Watching the swirl of darkness and neon behind him and listening to the click of signals for the streetlight at the intersection a few doors down a few seconds before the lights actually turned, counting the space of time in between the click and the actual light change because that is the one kind of space in the world I know best.

"She did make one comment more," I said.

He turned and for the briefest moment the dullness in his eyes was replaced by something else: a deeper dullness or a faint kind of hope or by curiosity of one kind or another.

"What did she tell you?" he asked. "Dammit, I knew she had more to say than you've told me. The impression I got from her was that the two of you had sat around chatting for hours. So let's have it."

"She said you mope. You sulk. You're listless. She said you were a goddamn bore."

His features jiggled ever so slightly, then fell back into place. For some seconds he continued to stare at me but the stare went through me and never reversed back upon himself.

"Anything else?"

"Nothing else," I said.

I went back inside the laundromat. My first machine was whining, kicking up a jitter from the floor, winding down from its last fast spin. I lifted the lid and the machine clicked and slowed and I quickly slammed the lid back down. It clicked back into its high spin gear immediately and for a moment I imagined the white enamel washer body enclosed me as well, that I was inside the unit, spinning, pressed back against the metal wall, all the moisture being forced out of me and that before long I might expect to be removed to a larger and warmer place where I would tumble and steam and at last be taken out all hot and static-popping so that I might be folded and tucked away in a closet underneath three air fresheners or placed in a chest with mothballs. There my life would close, a neat fold of arms, legs, head and torso in the undreaming dark: a few inches of Emancipated Woman now resigned to that sterile habitat, final release from the sins of my work in the Love Parlour.

It was the man in the tan suit who snapped me out of it. I heard his voice and opened my eyes to see myself leaning on my arms over the white closed top of the washer. I turned to him, smiling.

"Pardon me? What did you say?"

Maybe he saw something in the smile that was not meant to be there, or saw something else that he had already found too often. At any rate he backed up, caught between politeness and awkwardness, in that moment establishing as a fact that he too was the kind susceptible to the confusion and thwarted intention that can send one spinning.

"These machines," he said, "they all seem to be finishing at the same time."

"Yes," I told him, "that's the way it works."

The boy had climbed up on the table where the magazines were piled. He was pretending to be asleep, he announced, and his father asked him why his eyes were open.

"Because of tigers," the boy said.

I didn't find him amusing any longer. He was beautiful but full of himself, as boys are. Anyway it was past his bedtime and where, I wondered, was his mother?

I pulled over the wire roller car and emptied my wash into it. By the time I finished unloading one machine the next was waiting and so I went on down the line. I stacked the clothes in enormously high and I was afraid they'd fall to the floor so I asked the man in the suit if he would help me roll them over to the dryer. "Anything for a lady," he said.

We pitched the wet things in.

"Men are more romantic," he said. "I'll go home tonight and think about all the delicate underwear I've touched." He was very grim when he said this and not even looking at my underwear and I didn't bother to reply.

I slammed the heavy doors shut and rolled dime after dime into their warm inflated bellies.

The man in the suit became bored and took his child out to walk on the dark street. I sat on, reading the *Furioso* poem, deciding after the first few minutes that it wasn't much.

Prop up the corn,
shadow master.
Rouge your flesh
and dance,
for it is your blood
that seasons my time here.

At a quarter to eleven two young women in GI overcoats came in and retrieved their laundry from one of the still dryers. After that an elderly woman entered and rooted through the

78

Lost and Found basket for a while.

"This one is nice, don't you think?" she asked, holding up a single blue stretch sock, and I told her it was, so she walked out with it and two or three other things. A house painter appeared, wearing white splattered coveralls, muttered something apologetic, and pulled from no. 28 a pair of white coveralls identical to those he was wearing.

The man in the tan suit returned and transferred his clothes to the dryer. I asked him where his son was and he replied that the boy was asleep in the car. "Where's your wife?" I asked. "Out of the country," he said. "Way out." He gave me a sour look and I guess I gave him the same look back.

I got home at 11.45. The phone was ringing. I knew who it would be.

"I've left him," she said.

I didn't speak.

"They are such children, aren't they?" she said.

I waited for Rebecca to hang up.

"God," she said at last, sighing—"what a waste!"

That night I took the phone out of its jack. I didn't want to be on the receiving end of any more calls and I thought it likely Tom would be calling me. I put the chain on the bolted door and turned off all the lights too and dressed my bed with clean sheets in the dark. Then I took off my clothes and climbed in naked between the new sheets. I turned on the small bedside Sony and listened to quiet music for a time. Then I slept.

The sleep was deep and easy and I didn't think about anyone.

For the next several nights I didn't return to my apartment at all but stayed overnight with a friend whom I have been getting along well with lately.

I have yet to see Tom but yesterday I saw Rebecca on the street walking with a very striking man. They were holding hands and laughing. She was wearing his hat, a black fur thing that covered her ears. She went into a little dance when she saw me, and I crossed the street to avoid having to pass them.

My friend, whose name is Rufus, a silly name I know, tells me I've become callous and vindictive, two traits he does not admire in a woman.

"Only in women?" I ask, and he moves the subject on into other areas. It pleases him to think of me as a dangerous woman. For the moment it amuses him to search and define what exactly the danger is. It amuses me too because the danger isn't where he thinks it to be. He rolls over into my arms, in my bed now, and lodges his face at my neck. For a long time his breathing is all there is and then I begin to feel his tongue on my skin and his hand glides smoothly down my backside until it comes to rest against what he refers to specifically as my lonely mother's ass.

But it—the danger in me—isn't there.

It isn't there and though I'll respond soon enough it won't be found any place familiar to him or by any method or technique practiced on me in the past.

For Love of Madeline

Earlier this year, in the remote village of El Flores, in the state of Michoacán which is itself remote—in El Flores then, which is one of the many poor villages lying nearby to the big lake there (but creeping away from the water's edge in cozy and random turns up the mountain because they have long since learned to distrust the lake during the rainy season—which in El Flores is most of the year)—in El Flores, I say, there appeared one morning, tacked to four trees at the four corners of the Plaza Principal and to the green-crusted statue of Don Vasco around which the crumbling *jardín* is built, these hand-painted signs bearing the signature of the town's most noted citizen, Sr. Gómez:

TO THE PUBLIC

EMERGENCY SITUATIONS INVITED

DRAMATIC FORCEFUL PERSONALITY TIRING OF FAMILIAR BATTEL OF WILS SEEK SUBMISSIVE ENTROVERTED FAMALE TO SHARE LIFE OF LOVE WEALTH Y ADVENTURE. APPLY CAFE BODEGA.

The signs were displayed in such a manner that it was possible for one to read them from the outdoor tables of any of the three cafés looking onto the main plaza, and from the fourth side as well. Here stood the simple whitewashed cathedral and its few stalls selling candles and plastic saints and newspaper sheets which women—tourists, of course—with uncovered heads might occasionally rent for twenty centavos.

Madeline, a determined step or two ahead of her companion, Raymond, had read the signs this morning from all four sides, first while circling the plaza in an attempt to delay a decision as to which restaurant they might attend (and thus to delay breakfast which they could not afford or perhaps hoping by such malingering to circumvent the issue altogether), and again when she emerged—to the distress of Raymond, by the way—from the cathedral with the sheet of newsprint over her head. He resented the twenty centavo expense and insisted, rather querulously, that it was too late for prayer to do them any good. "Especially," he said, "—especially as we do not believe in God, anyway."

One might have seen Madeline's thin lips press her teeth, her pale, long arms whip out and wrench the paper into halves. Might have seen her, that is, turn on him in momentary rage, taking quick breaths that stopped short of her lungs and left her skin spotted, her fingers white. (Her tantrums as a child had been intense and regular and, let us say, successful; she was a nervous, opinionated girl, much inclined to quick fits even now.)

"Especially," said Raymond, who had long since ceased to be frightened of her, "—especially, as you are such a fool that God, if he did exist, would only laugh."

Madeline, as usual, had not favoured him with a verbal reply. She had hugged her stomach and marched off to the Bodega and sat down.

Now—and for some time now—the two of them had been

seated under the portico at the Bodega, Madeline sipping at water she suspected was impure, and Raymond engrossed in the news sheet—rehabilitated with great care—which he could not understand. He looked up, glancing at her, and now looking down at the lake which had risen during the night, volunteered his thoughts in a tired, petulant way: "I don't see why we have to eat here. I don't see why we couldn't go to the market and get a peso glass of juice or maybe a melon or some bananas that would cost practically nothing. I don't know what the hell you think we're going to do about lunch, not to mention dinner. It's times like these—I don't mind saying it— times like this, you gripe my ass."

Madeline shook her head gently, smiling in a polite way that either meant she was not listening to him or that she did not care what he did. The smile lingered, if only to annoy him, which fact Raymond realized as he let his gaze pass from lake to cathedral to plaza—as he let himself look anyplace but at her. He knew perfectly well why they were not again at the marketplace. Even its sight now made her ill. For the past five days she had been suffering a mild *turista*—the pain was not bad but neither would it leave her. Its small inconveniences had first embarrassed her; now the condition made her furious and she would clench her teeth, breathe her short breaths, when asked whether she felt better or worse.

I'll remain calm, the girl was thinking now. I won't let him know how much his very sight disgusts and infuriates me. She quietly stretched her hand out on the table beside the silver-ware which the waiter had brought long before. He had yet to bring the menu which Madeline was anxious for, wanting to see for herself what they could not afford.

As for Raymond, now that he had told her how he felt, he was perfectly content to sit. He believed that if only more peo-ple would sit and think and take life easy the world would be a far better place. He was, in fact, capable of believing that if he sat here long enough this morning, thinking and watching and taking life easy, then all their troubles would go away. It was largely this attribute—and Madeline's greed—that had reduced them to their present economic status. Between them they had sixteen pesos.

"Where we slept," said Raymond—but here he paused. A man in a white suit was drifting by, bowing, heavily ringed fingers clutching his lapels. "Where we slept," said Raymond, "it's under water now. But I don't suppose anyone has noticed."

Madeline did not reply. She was watching two ants on the table. The ants had thus far successfully moved a crust of bread from the centre to the ledge. A third ant had joined them for a while but she did not see it now. One of the two ants was now reconnoitering along the edge, seeking the best route down. Madeline picked up the bread crumb and returned it to the centre. She watched without expression as the two ants immediately began chasing about in broken directions. A fly on her elbow seemed to be watching them. I will not speak to him, the girl thought. I will not talk to him unless it becomes utterly necessary.

A man's shadow fell between their table and the sun.

"Mademoiselle has been to El Flores before?"

The polite, chivalric voice at an adjacent table made her turn. The fly on her arm lifted away and spun in the sun. The speaker, dressed in his white linen suit, stood tilted off his heels with one arm tucked high behind him. He was very tall for a native of the region—so Mady thought—and she waited to see his eyes which were shielded by a white sombrero.

"Mademoiselle would like perhaps the sights pointed out to her?"

He rocked on his heels and now slung the other arm behind him as well. Madeline could see enough of his face to ascertain the local bones and colouring. The mademoiselle to whom he spoke had raised one shoulder high about her neck. He might

84

not have been there at all—so her pose maintained—an obstruction between herself and the sun. She was eating a yellow melon and her hand, resting on the Cerveza portion of the Carta Blanca table top, gripped the base of a tall glass of orange juice as if she thought someone might want to take it from her.

"I might place me some signs too," Raymond said. He was staring off across the plaza at nothing in particular. "Wanted, one good ticket out of here. *Y no vuelta* either." His eyes swept lazily across the patrons seated at the other open-air cafés, and came to momentary rest on Madeline. She was now looking down Calle de Agua to where a fisherman sat with his feet drawn up under him, mending a butterfly net.

"They don't use those nets for fishing, you know," Raymond said. "It's strictly the tourist bit." He saw Madeline close her eyes, clenching her face tight. He watched to see how long it would be before she breathed. But then he remembered how much this sort of thing bored him and he looked instead at the ants. They had found the bread and now there were five of them. When he observed that Madeline's eyes were open again he reached forward and pressed a finger against the bread, crumbling it into numerous small pieces. He saw Madeline press her hands to her face and he stared a moment, considering whether she would cry.

"The Mademoiselles, they are desiring company, yes?"

The man in the white suit was now at another table where two middle-aged ladies sat with their backs to the plaza and the sun. They wore the El Flores rebozos, one orange and the other red, and the El Flores sandals made of white leather stapled crudely to rubber-tire soles. Their feet seemed very clean. "*This* Mademoiselle and *this* Mademoiselle, the situation is an emergency, no?"

Neither of the two ladies bothered to reply. They were waiting, too. In each of the three cafés around the plaza the norteamericanos were awaiting breakfasts, *desayuno*, which might, or might not, arrive.

"Wanted!" said Raymond, smiling and shaking the rigid shoulder of Madeline beside him, "—a one-way ticket the hell out of here!" She shook her shoulder free and adjusted her chair so that she might be just beyond his reach. The movement was not alone enough to satisfy, though she remained in this position briefly. Then she moved her chair again, straightened, and in a series of tight, violent stabs, swept ants and crusts to the floor. Raymond gave light applause.

The sun was suddenly obscured and both looked quickly to the sky—as did most other patrons seated in the cafés around the plaza. The cloud passed. It was too early—even for the rainy season—for rain. Across the way, at La Chica, on grounds leased from the Posado de Don Vasco, a bent woman with a black rebozo wrapped around what she claimed either to be her dead or sleeping child, was threading through the tables, her palms cupped to receive whatever centavos might be offered. A dark gentleman in rags, holding a tall tin cup such as those milk-peddlers employ, squatted at the entranceway, his feet bound by a clever arrangement of cloth, rope and twigs.

"Maybe we could get our dinero back from them," Raymond said. "You think we could?" His voice was soft, as if by such modulation he hoped to serve notice of his restraint. As if he meant to say, "You can worry but, as for me, I have nothing to worry about." Or perhaps he spoke softly only because the wind—and the situation—invited softness now.

"Three lousy pesos," said Madeline. She drank the last of the warm water in her glass to disguise her sneer. To drown the words her mouth yet could feel. She thought: God, I've done it now. Broken my silence, the last weapon I had. And replaced the glass, thinking: What a fool I am to talk to him.

But the man with her did not notice his victory. A young

86

Mexican in a grey, splattered Volkswagen was circling the plaza, the top of his head concealed behind the fringe of a red satin curtain that adorned each window. A plastic Jesus danced from the rearview mirror and a host of other such symbols were attached to a rear window pedestal. The car boasted a Michoacán plate but it was not an El Flores car. He circled the square a second time and pulled up now at the vacant taxi zone beside a sign clearly reading SE PROHIBE ESTACIONAR. He did not get out. A boy on the curb with a sponge and bucket stood regarding him.

"It is his first car today," Raymond said. "Ortega is not yet ready to go to work."

"That is not it at all," snapped the girl—her chair scraped over the tiled floor and several people, including the man in the white suit, turned to stare at her. "Ortega knows perfectly well that the man does not want his car washed."

It was Raymond's turn to sneer. "Why," he asked, leaning on an elbow toward the girl, "—why doesn't the man want his car washed?"

"That isn't the question," said Madeline—her voice snapped right and left and several of the Mexican men seated nearby were nodding their heads. "The boy isn't going to ask the man if he wants his car washed because the boy knows the Mexican hasn't got a peso between himself and hell." The men nearby were grinning and nodding though of course they had no idea what she was saying. "No more," said the girl, "than the three lousy pesos you gave those miserable beggars would stand between us and it, between us and anything else you could name." The men now grinned more widely and passed inaudible comment back and forth between themselves. They did not understand her—*No entiendo? No entiendo? Cómo?*—but before her period of unaccustomed silence they had seen her for many days waving her arms and slicing the air and spitting out a variety of sounds containing the name of her lazy friend,

87

Ramón.

They watched now to see in what maner he would respond —for sometimes he too would wave his arms and screech— but he was instead looking past the Café Alameda to Calle de San Francisco where now they looked too. A delegation of officials from the municipal building had emerged. Three of them wore suits that seemed made of glass, and the fourth, whose clothes did not reflect the sun, was gesturing vehemently.

The man in the white suit, to whom Madeline was giving her attention, was now seated alone at a table away from the sun. He had removed his hat—it rode vaquero-style on one narrow, quivering knee—but Madeline could not see his eyes. The jar of Nescafé Instantáneo had been brought him and he was stirring spoonfuls into a large white mug of steaming water.

The waiter passed through the tables and a number of people—norteamericanos—shouted for his attention, but he ignored them, again disappearing inside.

"Café negro, Café con leche—hell, just coffee," groaned Raymond, whose own voice had been among those calling for the boy. "You wouldn't think that's too much to ask."

"The Mademoiselle would see the sights?" the man in the white suit was saying to no-one, "—the Mademoiselle is perhaps only passing through? What does the Mademoiselle desire?"

Other patrons were drifting in and selecting tables or drifting in and standing a while and then drifting out again. Several of those who believed they had been waiting too long at the Bodega were drifting out to go and wait at another café, just as others from the Alameda and La Chica were quitting their tables to come here. The café owners found this practice reasonable: a customer gained for each customer lost. All who truly desired food at this time of day eventually would be served. Moreover, waiters at the Bodega, at La Chica, at the

88

Alameda would not grow restless and haughty and demand more pay, as they had different faces to serve each day. So long as their tips could not be correctly anticipated—so long as the waiters were happy and satisfied—why it might be some time —weeks perhaps—before they terminated their service with, say, the Bodega, for a more promising relationship with the Alameda or La Chica.

The man in the white suit understood all this—he acted like a man who did. Now pouring his hot milk from the ceramic jug, now stirring, now adding spoonfuls of coarse sugar. He was in no hurry. It was easy to see he was satisfied. The sombrero bucked vaquero-style on his thin knee, but not because he desired to go anyplace. Madeline, watching him, waited for him to drink, for then he might lift his face—but she was wrong for she saw him now dipping his mouth to meet the rim of the mug, sucking up the liquid between his teeth.

"The café is good, no? *Es bueno? Correcto? Buenas días,* Mademoiselle. The Mademoiselle is in the hot-seat, no?"

Madeline turned. There was no-one behind her. The man in the white suit was addressing his remarks directly to her.

"The Mademoiselle has desires? *Si?* The Mademoiselle is ambitious for the food?" He smacked his hand on the table edge, made a sucking noise with his tongue between his teeth —and immediately the waiter appeared. He lifted his fingers in a casual outward motion and the waiter nodded and hastened off, appearing a moment later with a single menu which he held to his chest until Madeline reached for it.

"Well, grass-uss," Raymond said, turning to the man in the white suit, "much-us grass-us, you know." The man shrugged and turned aside.

Along the cobbled street in front of the Bodega the municipal officials were passing. One or two citizens from the Alameda, from La Chica, the owner of the *zapatería,* and the moustached proprietor of the *peluquería*, had joined them. Now they had paused before the Bodega to invite companionship. *Cómo está usted?* The day is promising, no? We have been asking "Where are the clouds?" It is our intention now to walk to the water and measure its progress during the night. Someone has been saying the lean-to of the Americanos is washing out to sea? Can this be? We ask you! *Mañana*, what height will the water be? It is wise to be cautious, no? And only our duty as good citizens of El Flores. Who will go with us now?

No-one from the Bodega joined their group. Its composition was too official for their tastes and, yes, there was another matter. Most Bodega patrons had been looking across the plaza at the boy with the bucket who had at last approached the man who sat in the car behind the fringed red curtain. They could hear the boy's thin voice and the man's muffled response. The boy, whose name was Ortega, was saying he would watch the car. For a peso he would see no-one stole the hub-caps or the crooked antenna or perhaps even the license plate. For a peso he would watch it very good. The man was evidently inquiring what need he had of the boy's service when he was himself in the car and perfectly capable of maintaining his own vigilance over the machine. The boy was saying, "But, ah, you are sleeping much of the time. I could myself steal the hubcaps and the antenna and perhaps the license plate."

It seemed—to those watching from the Bodega—that the man in the grey car would have to give Ortega the peso if he wanted to get back to sleep again. Finally the boy got into the car with the man, and the man drove off with him—and none of the people in any of the three cafés understood this at all.

"Was that Ortega who got in the car?" they asked.

"No," they agreed, "it was someone else, for why would Ortega get in the car of the man from someplace else? No, it was not Ortega."

"We agree, yes," others added, "but if it was not Ortega who got in the car then where is he now? Where is his bucket and his sponge? No, it must have been Ortega who got in the car for otherwise his sponge and his pail would be near the fountain where they always are."

"Yes, it was Ortega who got in the car," they all could agree. After all, he had been seen talking to the man. And, after all, it was true that Ortega could never be counted on. He might very well have got in the car. He would return soon—in an hour or two—before nightfall—and say it was the Saint—El Santo from the cine and the comic book—who was in the car. A few kilometres out of El Flores they had put masks over their faces, and driven thus to other villages around the lake which were not so well prepared for the flood. Whose foolish officials had not had the presence of mind to stir from their chambers and go to measure the level of water. Possibly this very minute Santo and Ortega were pulling goats and cows and children and old men from the swollen lake.

"For that," they all agreed, "is the way Ortega passes the day when he isn't charging a peso for the car. And sometimes even then it is El Santo who pushes the sponge."

Raymond and Madeline had their breakfast by this hour—*bollillos* and *mermelada*—in the sun, to the clatter of dishes and the occasional lifted voice of someone in the street or in the plaza calling to someone in another place. The rolls were stale but they voiced no complaints. For the marmalade was good and more of it than they could eat. Only once did Madeline rush off to the *damas*, but she was soon back, submerging her irritation and the occasional acute pain in a bickerish concern for whether Raymond had eaten more than his share.

A small boy whose patched britches reached his knees loitered by, selling Chiclets which no-one bought. A man and a burro saddled with wood came by and stood for perhaps five minutes in the street between cathedral and plaza. When he had accomplished what he set out to do he slapped the flank of the donkey and both moved on a few yards to stand in another place. The cooks left for the market with their baskets and plastic bags, getting ready for the *comida* trade.

The breakfasting people sat on, their ranks thinning somewhat. Some moved to the stone benches on the plaza and some simply went away, while others moved from shade to sun to shade again. The municipal delegation alighted a second time from their red building on the Calle de San Francisco, proceeding with a second measurement of the water's depth, for it seemed no-one had recorded the first.

"The situation is perverse," they said. "*Obstinado,*" the men in the glass suits claimed. "For this, one must—*vigilar de cerca*—keep one's eye peeled!" True, the lake seemed not much higher now. "*Un poco, no más!*" True, the sky did not seem a threat now. But in the meantime—*en el ínterim*—they would keep their eyes peeled, for that was no more than wise. The fourth member continued from time to time to wave his arms excitedly.

The man in the white suit remained aloof from these manifestations of life in El Flores—remained enchanted, or so it appeared, as now and again he might rise and journey about the tables, seeing to this or that Mademoiselle's health, her desires, extending his good hopes, proffering his services. Enchanted, yes, for it gave him not the slightest pause that the ladies inevitably turned their shoulders to him, shielded their faces, allowed no exchange, uncivil or otherwise, to escape their lips. He sat now with one white boot at rest on the black stand of the shining, brass-edged box of the small shoeshine boy whose own shoes were very dirty. The boy maintained a scowl of deep concentration, his tongue caught between his lips. He had a scab on his ear and infrequently a white hand would shoot up and flick at it as if dislodging flies. The man's sombrero rested low over his eyes; his white coat, meticulously folded, stretched across his lap.

Madeline's companion, Raymond, had left his table—had gone and come and gone again. He was making trips to the bank—the Banco Nacional on the other side of the plaza—and reporting back his progress there. He had been awaiting —they had been awaiting—a cheque for many days now.

"They've got it," Raymond would say. "I know they have. My bank tells me they sent it! Of course the Banco Nacional has it. Oh, they're so corrupt, so inefficient! But they've got it, I know they have. I'll have them tear up the place until they find it—where else could it be!"

To these assertions—to his meek eyes which said to her, "Isn't it true? Don't you find it reasonable, this that I say?"— to these Madeline merely returned a gaze of bleak sobriety that lent all the more force to her feelings of indolent outrage. There *was* no cheque. She shifted her chair once more that the sun might not shine directly in her face; she sighed and turned and averted her eyes; she scratched her shoulder and rubbed her lids and wrestled about in the chair until she sat just so... waiting for him to be gone again... waiting to see him trot off across the square and circle the statue of Don Vasco and jump the rock wall there where the sign read EXCLUSIVO SITIO NO ESTACIONARSE. Waiting to see him disappear one more time into the apologetic confines of the Banco Nacional. There *was* no cheque. There would *be* no cheque. There had never *been* a cheque. And if the man in the brown suit repeated *Sí, Sí, mañana, por cierto mañana*, as she had heard him do, then that man was a fool—though perhaps no more than she had been.

She got up now and moved to another table, away from her nest of breadcrumbs and marmalade which had been accumulating flies. She watched the man in the white suit spit on his fingers and relay the spit to his shoes, in apparent dissatisfaction with their glossy shine. The sky struck dark again but the overcast was temporary; the sun was bold behind it and the wind was churning the clouds along at such speed that she could feel the shadows changing on her face. "Wanted," she said to herself, "one good word from the Banco Nacional."

"Wanted," she continued under her breath, "—one good wanted, want wanting wanted now." The speech surprised her: she rarely talked gibberish and never to herself. But there are times, she thought—this might be one of them—when gibberish accomplishes where all else fails. She fixed her shoulder straps and slipped her broad feet into the Cuernavaca sandals and rose from the table. She turned her face a quick moment into the passing edge of sun, blinked, and knotted her fists at her side—and walked over to the table of the man in white who was just then saying to three ladies waiting for the *cajero* to take their money:

"Mademoiselle can perhaps explain. The Mademoiselles would like perhaps the sights to see them now?"

She came to stand between the ladies and the man. The ladies were nervous, bleached, new to El Flores. Their money fluttered like lazy hands.

"Señor Gómez?"

The sun, obscured though it might be, was hot on the side of her face and a fly was crawling on her neck—or perhaps it was sweat. She had the taste of marmalade in her mouth. She waited for the man to tilt his sombrero back and raise his head and look at her. The three ladies drifted away, chatting amiably—laughing now.

"Good morning, yes?" the man inquired of Madeline, in his polite, chivalric voice, "—you have business, no?" He tilted the sombrero back and elevated his head but Madeline saw that his eyes were closed.

She sat at his table, let her elbows fall, hooking her fingers behind her neck.

"You are fine, yes?" he said. His lips curled into a contemptuous smile. "It is good to see you again. Have you improved?

No more the *turista*, no? Is there yet the difficulty with your friend's money at the bank?" He waved the jewelled fingers across his face and smiled, saying, "Ah these banks! They have no humanity, no finer sensibilities, do you think?"

The girl waited for his eyes to open. She thought if ever he would open his eyes and she could see into him—his character, his soul—she could believe she was doing this. She had quite forgotten that such sighting had never served her well. She leaned close now, whispering: "I've come about the position." She moistened her lips and spoke again: "In response to your ad." She saw his mouth widen—he tilted back his chair and transferred the sombrero to his knee.

"But how unfortunate," he murmured. "How do you say it, that the position is filled."

She watched his closed lids; she could see his eyes quivering and the spread of blue veins in the skin. His cheeks held the faintest touch of red, as though they might have been lightly brushed with rouge. The chair legs came down and she felt his hand fall heavily on her thigh. "Ah, but the business is concluded, you see. How regrettable! If I had known! For the emergency situation is intolerable, believe me, I am a man who knows. *Lo siento*, Mademoiselle. I am sorry but, as you say it, my hands are tied. You see?"

The girl saw very well. She had been watching him all morning, no-one else had talked to him. It was the game he would play. Raymond, too, had his games.

They sat on together. The sun climbed and the Plaza Principal filled and the *comida* crowd began wandering in. The paths of those from the Alameda, from La Chica, from the Bodega, intersected; gossip and news and speculations were exchanged. The lake, it was established now, was very definitely on the rise. Already its rim was touching the first stones of Calle de Agua. The man from the *oficina de telégrafo* was rumoured to have said that three of the more distant villages on the lake were now totally submerged, but this was scoffed at for the man from the *telégrafo* had a weakness for pulque and moreover the service had never been so fast before. Now and then a man would run down and squat on his heels, testing the water's depth—a mimic of the municipal officials—and his friends would laugh and enact similar tests themselves. The odd child stood around its edge tossing rocks or sticks or dung into the cloudy water. Many others were arriving, too, to observe at close hand the lake's rising. The *helados* vendor bypassed those seated in the plaza and pushed his cart down Calle de Agua, while behind him trudged the weathered *chicharones* man, bound in rags, conveying on his head the large basket of fried porkskins and his bottles of chili sauce. The sky darkened and no-one appeared to take offense.

Madeline and the man in white had nothing to say about this quickening along their front. At one point she moved out of her lethargy, her despair, long enough to grasp his arm and thereby claim his attention once more. "But what if it doesn't work out?" she demanded. "What if you find you can't get along with this person you've taken on?"

The three bells in the three steeples of the church on the plaza toned midday—or some such hour. In El Flores one could never be sure. In another minute—in another five or ten —the more festive bells of San Antonio on the mountainside would reply.

"It might not, you know," Madeline said. She released his arm and settled back in her chair. "American girls don't like to take a lot of shit."

The man grinned. For the first time, Madeline saw into his eyes. "Ah," he said, "but in that event I will have an opening, yes?" He let her go on looking; he let her see what she would see. Then he rose from his table, blinked, gave her a despondent leer—and walked out of the Bodega, bowing wide to the tables, saying, "Mademoiselle will forgive? The Mademoiselles are satisfied?"

She watched him go. She watched him take the steps of the *jardín*, circle the statue of Don Vasco, saunter at leisure down the walkway with its erratic growth of weed and flower—watched him sweep gracefully up the next series of steps and ascend into the winding Calle de la Noche de la mil Lunas. She expected him to turn and wave, to turn and lift his hat, but he did not. He rounded a turn and was gone.

She exhaled, bore down heavily on the arms of her chair. "He'll take me," she said aloud. "He has to, he has no-one else." She continued looking up Calle de la Noche de la mil Lunas. The street emptied into the mountains and there at its top a black cloud had settled. Any minute now the rain would come, perhaps it was already raining up there. Earlier, she had seen Raymond—or believed she had—threading his way carefully up the street of moons with his green backpack filled and their last ten pesos in his pockets. But possibly not. Possibly he was yet in the bank, bluffing the manager with his talk of a cheque that would never come. It was even conceivable—it was not entirely out of the realm of possibility—that any moment now he would come racing across the plaza, waving in his hands more than enough money to take them away from El Flores.

Possible—remotely so—but not likely. In all probability he was up on the mountain now, waving his thumb. Looking out for a man in a grey car. Saying good riddance to all that. Saying to himself, "What a hassle that Madeline was!"

She prayed for rain. She hoped the rain would thunder down and wash him in a panic off the road.

On cue, the rain came. It thundered down, whipped about by a simultaneous rising of wind. It drove over stones and pelted trees and formed a thick screen over the lake. It drove El Flores—it even drove Madeline, eventually—indoors. Where she remained for perhaps an hour, perhaps more, as the rain did not abate. One might have seen her finally—a

97

lean, white girl, clothes adhering to her frame—streaking across the plaza in the falling rain, bounding up the steps of the cathedral and shaking its thick dark doors which of course were now closed to give the building protection against the wind and rain. And now turning, fleeing up the street of moons, slipping on the wet, gushing stones—banging her knees, wiping rain from her face as she ran—but coming at last to the famous tinsel-sheeted door of Sr. Gómez. Might have seen her, I say, knocking her frail fists against the door—cursing—though the wind and rain took her cries and the door remained closed. For so it was earlier this year before the lake washed over El Flores and made it into another place.

For Love of Eleanor

They met, as was their custom, on the sunny side of the Plaza Principal and crossed in silence over the ruined grounds, passing on their way the attendant *policia* who stood guard over the tiled fountain, for no-one was to use it anymore. The young policeman murmured the usual greeting of the morning, inclining an emaciated shoulder toward Eleanor, who returned the courtesy with a smile at his vague face and rumpled uniform, while at her side Frank remained absorbed, watchful of where he stepped, for yesterday he had soiled his shoes. It was clear from his expression—clear to Eleanor at any rate, and to the policeman who no doubt shared his view—that he found El Flores now altogether a dreary and disgusting place.

Quite content herself, Eleanor placed her arm lightly on his as they walked together down the high plaza steps toward the Café Bodega, where they came every morning now for the most extended breakfast in all of Mexico.

"Shall we sit outside?" asked Frank, "or is it too cool for you?" Sometimes it was too cool for her and sometimes it was not, though Frank would have been the first to say that where they sat seemed rarely to be determined by the temperature.

"Oh, outside, of course," replied Eleanor, "there is so much to see." Frank released her arm, groaning inwardly at this display of her good nature—now stepping politely aside to allow her to pass in front of him through the roped entrance to the Bodega. It was a simple hemp rope the Bodega's owner, Señor Gómez, had installed only the previous week, either as a symbolic effort to cordon off his restaurant from the cruel malady attacking the rest of the village or, more likely, as a gesture of discouragement for his many customers who preferred to quit the premises without paying their bills. In any event, Eleanor admired the new rope. It was the same rope that Michoacán peddlers used to secure their goods as they moved from market to market, the same one the local *leñadores* used to bind wood to their donkeys for transport to the houses of the rich *Americanos*. She had seen it restraining the huge alfalfa bundles that the peasants carried on their backs and she had even occasionally seen it holding up a workman's pants. It was a very useful rope and it did succeed, to her mind, in giving a certain class to this drab and sexless café.

She took a seat just by the sidewalk and immediately leaned into the leather harness of the chair, closing her eyes to the sun, which for the moment was bright and warm. She pushed the sunglasses up into her hair and drew the fiery red rebozo close around her neck. Frank accepted the chair opposite her, relieved to see her so soon settling down. Perhaps this morning they could have a breakfast without hysterics or posturing or Eleanor's undiminished fascination with death. He was more than a little tired of Eleanor and this morning felt—not without some pride—a physical depletion as well.

But he was accustomed to speaking to Eleanor with his own wry brand of accumulated humour, and this morning did not know how to begin their conversation any other way. Thus he shifted about uncomfortably in his chair—it was too small for him—glanced about at the deserted tables, and inquired of Eleanor how her breakdown was coming along.

Eleanor sighed.

A cadre of soldiers passed in sloppy, near-silent formation in front of the café and Frank hoped Eleanor wouldn't open her eyes until they were gone. They would be going to the lake, of course, to relieve other soldiers standing guard there for no-one was to use the lake water either. He watched them until they had disappeared, and then he watched the dust settle behind them. He had heard the rumour—though apparently Eleanor had not—that last night the soldiers had been obliged to shoot someone, for naturally the people of El Flores had to have water and not all could be convinced that the lake was now contaminated too.

He noticed Eleanor move, the quick shaking of her head as if to dislodge the stubbornness of some thought or dream. "My breakdown, Frank," she said, "isn't quite what I had hoped for." She leaned forward, placing her hand on his arm in one of those tender gestures of domesticity which were so familiar to him and of which he so much approved. "No," she said smiling, "I was much happier in my other life, although it was far less interesting. What does one do with a breakdown? Nothing at all—the breakdown, sad to say, is doing it all to me."

Frank withdrew the cigarette package from his breast pocket and extracted one. He laid the cigarette down on the table top and stared at it dubiously, disheartened by this reminder that he had no more of his usual brand. He had never told her so, but he found Eleanor's breakdown more than a little boring.

"You see," said Eleanor, "in my present state I'm not responsible for my actions." Her voice lifted in laughter and Frank looked calmly about to see if anyone was watching.

The Bodega remained deserted.

A lone soldier walked casually up Calle de Agua and passed across the plaza, but while Eleanor viewed his progress with a slow twist of her head she refrained from speaking either about this soldier or about those others last night who had fired on the man who wanted water.

"Which means, dear Frank," she said, "that I am now cured!" Once again she laughed, though quietly this time, rather like a lady, and Frank stared rudely at her exposed teeth, which were perfect.

He offered her a cigarette which she refused, though she picked up the book of matches and lit his.

She deflamed the match by closing her mouth over it.

"I am not amused," said Frank, in the voice he would have used with his daughter. He jerked the matchbook from her hand and immediately arranged on his face his expression of offended gloom. He vividly recalled that earlier in the year, seated in the lobby of the Posado de Don Vasco across the way, she had lit another match and held it at her white neck until her hair had burst into flames and he had been forced to grab at her and shove her head into his stomach. Only then did he learn she was wearing a wig, for she had slid free of it to stand pointing and giggling at his astonished face as he stood clutching the wig under his smouldering jacket.

"Are you envious, Frank?" she was saying now, "—would you like a breakdown, too?"

He pushed back his chair and stood. "I can't afford it," he said—and stalked off to search for Gómez or the waiter.

But Gómez' small, odd office behind the cash register was empty and no-one was in the kitchen, although there may have been, for he only made a quick search from the door. He had a need—and cause, he reasoned—to preserve his innocence of Mexican kitchens.

He returned to find Eleanor taking the sun, resting her legs on his chair, her head pitched back, and her eyes shut tight. He adjusted the red rebozo judiciously over her shoulders, and applied a fatherly kiss to the top of her head. Then he lifted her legs to the floor, dusted the chair seat, and sat down.

He was content for some time to sit quietly watching her,

thinking: *ah, sweet Eleanor, how odd she is now!* . . . quite forgetting that she had been that way from the beginning: sweet and odd and rather fragile and, to him, quite ridiculously impenetrable. Her head swayed from side to side occasionally—beautifully, thought Frank—as if to music—and now and then he allowed a smile as her tongue flicked out and licked over her lips which he had always thought of as too thin but which he saw now were quite regular. He found it curious that she no longer used make-up on her face and that the face which he had once believed to be quite regular with its pink powders and mascara and tinted lips now looked rather lovely with all that removed. It was, however, the fine sweep of her shoulders that he most admired. Eleanor's shoulders—so he once had been informed—belonged in a museum, high on a pedestal with a glass frame and surrounded by a moat of intense flames.

A cool Indian, he thought now—it was a damned shame that she insisted on making life miserable for those who really were quite fond of her and had only her best interests at heart. It really was too bad—so Frank believed—what Eleanor had let happen to herself.

He saw that Eleanor had her eyes open now, and looked where she was looking: toward the carved, high, bolted doors of the Church of Our Lady of the Saints which Eleanor had lately taken to calling the El Flores headstone. The entire plaza had a mood of disenchanted isolation, though the mood was not confined to the plaza alone and indeed included the whole of the village. For one thing, they could see now the quiet preparations of the mourners at the *funeraría* up Calle de la Noche de la mil Lunas—the Street of Moons, as it was called —and the occasional mourner in his sinister black outfit crossing Calle de la San Francisco with flowers to deck the coffin mounts.

To his surprise Eleanor still did not speak of the death that was all around them. "Dear, dear Frank," she was saying now, smiling gaily across at him, "how is it I have come to know you so well! This morning you have that insufferable gloating air. It amounts almost to an odour, though I know you bathe. Was it the company you had last night?"

Frank was not annoyed. On the contrary he admitted to some mild pleasure or even pride in these absurd little insights of hers.

"Why, yes," he told her, "I did have company last night. An interesting girl, very odd, very sweet. I met her at Maya's opening."

Eleanor slid lower in her chair and for a moment Frank could hear her breathing—that peculiar way she became sometimes when excited—her mouth open wide, her breath shallow and so tentatively deepening that small white patches surfaced on her skin. "Oh, yes, Maya," she said at last. "That man who paints the dead!" Her voice was light, even somewhat tipsy, and Frank didn't want to talk about Maya or his see-through portraits of the dead.

"It wasn't a bad opening," he admitted begrudgingly, irritated that Eleanor might think he had attended for anything other than the punch and the people he would see. Over the next several minutes he proceeded to tell her who had been there, what they were wearing, and how they had behaved, about the strong, warm punch and the last-minute difficulties the gallery had experienced with the authorities who had removed all their ice—not caring that Eleanor displayed no interest, ignoring her when she loosened the top buttons of her El Flores blouse and flung the red rebozo aside that her white throat and freckled chest might have the sun.

Then he told her about the girl.

"But why," asked Eleanor when he had finished, proving that she had been listening all the while—"why was she asked to leave?"

"She insulted Maya's wife."

"I didn't know he was married," said Eleanor, finding the thought strange. "What did your girlfriend say to her?"

"She wasn't my girlfriend at that point," corrected Frank. "No, she told Maya's wife that the reason Maya didn't paint the living was because she, meaning Maya's wife, was as good as dead herself."

"That sounds pretty mild."

"Oh, I don't know. The woman isn't very attractive. She's not very smart either. And she kept Maya away from the punch. In all the time that I was there I never saw a flicker of emotion on her face."

"She sounds a lot like you," said Eleanor with a smile. "But they kicked your girlfriend out for that?"

"No," explained Frank. "It was after she insulted Maya. She told him that she didn't like the way he painted the dead."

"What did Maya say?" asked Eleanor, who was very interested in this.

"Nothing. He doesn't talk much. Not that she gave him much time. She told him what she didn't like about his paintings of the dead is that he faked it up too much. She didn't like his crummy—that was her word—his crummy symbolism, all those hot red roses crushed in the hands, and such. But finally what she found most detestable was that his dead people didn't look dead—that if you opened their eyes and put a fleck of colour in their cheeks they would look pretty much like everyday, normal, living people."

"I didn't know you liked the outspoken type," Eleanor said quietly.

"I don't approve of Maya's work," said Frank. "I don't see any point in painting the dead."

"That's too bad," smiled Eleanor, patting his hand. "You'd make a very worthy subject."

Frank turned his blank stare on her and they sat in pensive

silence until Eleanor picked the story up again.

"So naturally when she left you left with her because you were one of those without an orchid or a red rose in your hands —no doubt because both your hands were filled with all the tequila cocktails you could carry."

Frank did not take this comment seriously, though he was amused by the suspicion that Eleanor still expected some kind of physical loyalty from him.

"So that's Nora Meyer Jones," he concluded. "A cool Indian, I think you'll agree."

"Oh I agree," replied Eleanor, avoiding his eyes. "I'm always delighted when you can find someone who will sleep with you."

For a long spell neither had much more to say. The waiter did not enter, nor did the owner Gómez—nor for that matter did any other customer. All this solitude was quite extraordinary and it occurred to Frank to wonder whether others in El Flores knew something that he did not. Across the plaza two sentinels took up positions by the copper-sheeted doors of the Banco Nacional, though why they should want to he could not guess. A child, the boy Ortega who washed the cars of the *turistas* during better times, came to stare gloomily at the policemen holding watch over the fountain at the plaza's centre, but he soon trotted away, and the policeman completed his lazy turn around the fountain, the butt of his weapon dragging heavily at his heels. The street around the plaza was fixed with dry scales of mud, as were the elevated cobbled sidewalks and steps and the lower façades of certain shops. Here and there even now were derelict puddles of water whose scummy surfaces were like strange, flat jewels reflecting back the sun. The trees in the plaza, once so perfectly sculpted and planted in such manner that they formed a roof over the grounds, were depressingly open and contorted now, ragged and heavy with their coated dust. The stone benches formerly so neatly aligned

106

and securely anchored to the plaza green sat today aslant of their moorings, broken and crumbling; the brilliantly tiled, arched pavilion on which the musicians played for official functions had been entirely washed away. Down Calle de Agua toward the beach the hard mud thickened, its grey surface marred by countless projections that had been abandoned as the lake waters had at last, a week go, receded.

Frank, of course, was thinking of Nora Meyer Jones whom he had left asleep on the bed in his apartment. He had become almost totally immune to the ugliness, the grief, the desolation, the sense of inexhaustible doom embracing the whole of the village. Like Eleanor, he retained barely any memory of El Flores as it had been prior to the rain and the lake's inundation —poor and not yet altogether despoiled, timeless and rather lovely—no more than he, or either one of them, could acknowledge anything more than the most illusory of connections with or attachments to their previous life together. Their past lives had simply vanished since their arrival in El Flores, in much the same way that El Flores had itself now been largely obliterated.

Eleanor's thoughts were of the man from Guadalajara who painted the dead. She got up now and went briskly into the Bodega's kitchen where she found a bin of stale *bolillos* that the flies had no interest in. She put three of them on a plate and set about finding where Gómez kept his *mantequilla* or, more likely, the *margarina*. She found the butter unwrapped in a dish by the sink with flies swarming over it. The flies were quite listless and many of them she had to wipe aside. She ate the first roll, looking out from the darkness of the kitchen at Frank, who was looking at his nails, and over his shoulder at the young policeman at the plaza's centre, who had now leaned his rifle aside and was seated hunched over on the fountain wall. She had never met Maya but did have an acquaintance with his work. Maya, she felt sure, could find the death in both of them.

A few minutes later she returned to their table, carrying a beer tray that held two cups of instant coffee and a platter piled high with crusty *bolillos*. She had deliberately left the butter behind, out of amusement rather than malice, for she knew that it did not matter to Frank what he had for breakfast so long as someone else placed it before him. He had always taken considerable pleasure in having women deliver food to him.

He immediately halved a roll and bit into it, and turned to Eleanor. "She's a cool Indian," he began, "but it goes without saying that she doesn't have a peso to her name." Eleanor laughed, as he had known she would. They had enjoyed many of their closest moments together while discussing the various reasons why rich women were never attracted to him.

The sun had passed under and she dropped her sunglasses into Frank's pocket.

The bells in the three steeples at the head of the plaza tolled the tenth hour.

Around the corner from the Banco Nacional a beggar could be seen picking at refuse in the gutter.

They could see, at the *funeraría* on the hill, the health officers dispatched from Morelia in deep argument with the owner-undertaker whose establishment, it was being said, was not burying the dead with sufficient speed nor quite deep enough.

The less guttural bells of San Antonio on the mountainside responded to those in the plaza, and Frank pushed back his sleeve to check the time. "Only ten minutes late," he told Eleanor. The procession of mourners—the advancing of the dead, as Eleanor liked to think of it—was further behind than that. For the past several days the march had begun each morning at nine.

The sun came out again and Eleanor reclaimed her glasses,

placed them over her nose and leaned back to receive the sun.

"You've changed, Eleanor," said Frank.

Eleanor replied that yes she had.

"I mean your glasses," he said. "These are so much more glamorous than those you used to wear."

"Yes," said Eleanor, "I look ten years younger now. How old am I, Frank?"

"Thirty, I believe you said. Twenty-nine? As I recall, the last time we talked about it you weren't sure."

A boy wearing a dirty sarape that dragged at his heels came by and stopped in front of the Bodega to stare at them. He held a black, wet pig in his arms and the pig didn't move and Eleanor was correct in supposing that the pig was dead. She noticed that the policeman was no longer at his station by the plaza fountain and she missed his enfeebled presence there.

"Thirty-one?" suggested Frank. "You weren't sure."

He was himself 45.

"I'm always sure," said Eleanor, "down to the last decimal. The trouble is I never know when to stop counting. What year is this, Frank? Is this the year 1963?" She held her smile for him, wanting to see if he would remember that was the year they had married.

"This is the year 1973," replied Frank. "It is the year of hope and innocence and reduced prosperity. It is the year of the Watergate and the year for Nora Meyer Jones and for Frank and perhaps for you, Eleanor. It is also the year death came to El Flores."

"*El Santo es loco,*" murmured Eleanor, "*El Santo es——*". . . but she couldn't recall the phrase heard so often during these recent days. The Saint is insane, the Saint is evil-intentioned. For in the minds of the citizens of El Flores their patron saint had entered into El Diablo's fearful skin.

The boy with the dead pig finally went on.

"That's what I mean," continued Eleanor, "about not knowing when to stop counting. In my dreams the calendar never exactly specifies. But I believe I'm 28. I feel 28. Is 28 a good age, Frank?"

"It's a lovely age," laughed Frank. "I am myself 28."

"At any rate," said Eleanor, "it's a nice age for a breakdown."

With that she turned mopish and secretive and Frank shoved the *bolillos* aside and put on his own dark glasses. Beyond the Plaza Principal up Calle de la Noche de la mil Lunas at the *funeraria* the mourners at last had assembled. They numbered 50 or so at the moment but their ranks would swell as they filed down from the hill. Up there too, if they looked, Frank and Eleanor could see the odd, unattended child at play in piles of rubble. Such piles were numerous: up there and down Calle de San Francisco and Calle de Agua and around the wide street which squared the plaza and in the plaza itself. In the beginning municipal workers had arranged neat mounds of material from street stones uprooted or displaced, but for days the mounds had remained, awaiting instructions from the *funcionarios* to the men as to how exactly they should go about repairing the wrecked streets and walks, the eroded walls and various impaired buildings, though at last the rains quit and the lake receded and thus there seemed no need for hurry. The original purpose of the mounds became subverted, was forgotten as citizens of the village could see no good reason why they shouldn't empty their ruined possessions and all else they had no use for onto these official mounds. In a period of days all manner of refuse, unaccountable debris aswim in sewerage and stagnating mud, came to form these piles, and over them by the heat of day the insects swarmed and in their hot chambers the maggots bred. So the brackish decaying piles smothered through the week of sun, now sombre landmarks for Eleanor and the painter Maya to enjoy.

Eleanor nodded her head toward the plaza, "Pancho Villa returns," she announced.

For Gómez, the man in white, was advancing across the *jardín*. This morning, against the background of ruin and decay, he seemed more outlandishly impeccable than ever, a vision in his bold linen suit and white boots and wide sombrero. The girl, Madeline, who had been abandoned in El Flores a few weeks before and who now was in his employ, tagged listlessly behind him, her head bowing low either from her humiliation or because it was her present mood. He stopped, waiting for her, and when she was abreast of him he gave her a shove. A few days earlier she would have screamed at him, attacked him with her fists—now she acceded, whimpering, to his demands. It was not known what Gómez did to break haughty American girls; they came to him out of sorrow or need or because they had nowhere else to go and when he had crushed them he would give them a little money and send them on. Now he stood at the fountain, dipping a white handkerchief into the water; he passed the handkerchief to Madeline and pushed back his sombrero and allowed her to pat the wet cloth against his brow. He waved a hand of greeting at Eleanor and Frank seated at his table.

The sound Frank made was almost a snarl, which encouraged Eleanor to reply as she did.

"That man is beautiful. I adore Sr. Gómez."

Frank cursed for the first time that morning. He considered the man unsound and dangerous and certainly evil. It was rumoured that the man made his money from a string of prostitutes in Mexico City and Frank believed it. "Madeline is a fool," he said. "Surely Gómez is not the sole solution to her problem." He did not bother to inform Eleanor that Madeline had first come to him.

Both turned their attention to the thin American girl wiping the lips of the señor. She had long, straight hair and a strong, squarish chin but everything else about her Gómez had altered. He had taken her out of her homemade frocks, her sandals and levis or heavy-hanging gowns, and put her in the clothes he preferred. This morning she wore tight nylon shorts, high blue socks, and a matching blue nylon shirt open to display the Aztec medallion looped around her neck.

She looked, as Frank whispered to Eleanor, like a cross between a Catholic schoolgirl and a New Orleans whore.

But Gómez had not yet succeeded in doing much about her expression. She still had her contemptuous scowl and eyes that conveyed her attitude of imprisoned fury.

"You needn't be upset on her behalf," said Eleanor. "All her life Madeline has been looking for a way to be deprived."

Frank said nothing. Women, in his view, were to be ruled —some of them were even to be squandered—but only a criminal would want to deprive them of those qualities that were rightly theirs.

"Actually," continued Eleanor, "they are quite happy together."

"Oh, I never suggested they didn't understand each other," replied Frank.

"It's a beautiful relationship," smiled Eleanor.

"Like yours and mine," whispered Frank, and this time he was the one to smile.

The señor and Madeline were now approaching, hand in hand. Shadowed momentarily by the sun, his dark body seemed to recede and vanish inside his white clothes.

"What does he do with them," asked Frank, "when he has no more use for them?"

"Yes," Eleanor whispered back, "that would interest you."

The Mexican entered with a flourish, bowing low to all the vacant tables, spreading his arms, and addressing the empty chairs in his customary way: "The Mademoiselle would see the sights? The Mademoiselle is perhaps only passing through? At your service, please, what does the lovely Mademoiselle desire?" He careened gracefully through, clicked his heels in recognition of Frank, and bent to kiss the hand Eleanor was already offering him. The señor was always enthusiastic, he examined his women friends with zealous attention to their moods and whims. *"Ola, Ola, buenas días,* Mademoiselle, *muy bonita!*—and Death, how is your good friend Death this morning?"

Eleanor giggled, shifting her shoulders free of his oiling hands. The girl Madeline swept on inside without a word, securing herself inside Gómez' tiny office with a defiant bang of the door.

"Ola señor! Con su permiso?" He sat down, immediately launching forward to place his hands over Eleanor's knees and wedge his own between them. "But only one death during the night, Mademoiselle, *uno y no mas!"* He grinned roguishly, though his voice was more urgent than mocking. "Perhaps our amigo Death is ready to—how do I say it?—*echar pelillos a la mar!*—to bury the hatchet, no!" His hands slid back and forward along Eleanor's thighs. Her eyes gloated, misty from a feeling near to gratitude. She adored Gómez for his sinister vigour, his perverted chivalry. "Our sainted devil! *Qué mal suerte!* He is tired, no! So many to have died!" He rose, trembling with pleasure, bowing all around. *"Hasta luega, qué se diviertan*—enjoy yourselves!" He spun on his heels and crossed briskly to the office door which they had all heard Madeline bolt from inside. He knocked politely, rattled the knob.

"Go screw yourself," Madeline replied. Her tone was controlled and remorseless, schooled by years of privileged bitterness.

The Mexican grinned apologetically to Frank and Eleanor, spun a finger at the side of his head, and disappeared into the Bodega kitchen.

"With thousands of superb restaurants in this country," observed Frank with no more than a trace of irritation, "and thousands of fine villages, I sometimes wonder how it is I come to be here."

Eleanor was silent. Whenever Gómez went away something akin to her own sanity went with him.

The procession of mourners was now advancing in slow broken ranks down from the *funeraría* high on the Street of Moons. The white-washed portico under which they sat and which lidded the row of shops thrusting out to their left and centre seemed to her eyes amazingly clean above the shadowy business fronts and the *jardín* rubble. All the shops were closed, the *zapatería* and the *sombrerería* stall and the *peluquería* where Frank went each week to get his hair looked after. Café La Chica was barred and the Alameda across the way had numerous CERRADO signs attached to its front, as if its owner could not close his restaurant often enough. The *tienda* was closed and the *ropa* where Eleanor had bought her blouse, and *la papeleria* and the tailor's narrow hall.

One of the priests many assistants had come out and unbolted the doors of the cathedral and another had appeared and bolted it again.

The shining black and windowed coffin mounts that the mourners would be conveying were as yet hidden away. The procession was now perhaps a hundred strong, wrapping forlornly down the sinewy street, now appearing, now disappearing, while the buildings blended along that height, their walls in the sunlight a single climbing panel of faint pastels. The clay roofs seemed joined, a vibrant orange ceiling swimming gently over the town.

Madeline unlatched the office door and glanced around for a sight of Gómez and locked herself away again with a brief, violent curse.

The quiet shuffling footbeat of the approaching mourners fell and rose and was obscured again. They would not begin their dirge until they rounded the plaza corner and the cathedral stood in view.

Eleanor, with a slim elegant finger was spelling out the Carta Blanca beer legend on the table top. "Yes," she said, "and your girl last night, the cool Indian, is she very young?" Her voice was elegiac, remote and wan, although the expression on her face was vacant, simple-minded even, as if her thoughts were of nothing more significant than the flies across the room or a spot of water on her blouse.

"Twenty," Frank said. "On either side of twenty, I would guess. Attractive, somewhat large—very self-assured. She may be joining us, I hope you don't mind."

"No, I don't mind," answered Eleanor.

"But then again," said Frank, "she might not." He grimaced slightly to show Eleanor how matters stood. He was past that age when he could speak with confidence of women's intentions.

"Do you like her?" asked Eleanor.

Frank considered the question carefully. He didn't want to do an injustice to either of the women. "It's a temporary relationship," he said. "Nothing will come of it."

"Why, Frank, how can you say that? How can you be sure! She might prove to be your golden girl, the one you've been waiting for! You might grow to love her, to pine away when she isn't around, the two of you might in fact become inseparable, you might marry and have a host of wonderful children!"

Frank laughed. He leaned back in his chair and laughed, beaming at Eleanor's crude display of mirth. "I like that, Eleanor," he said. "I like that 'host of children' business! As if I will ever have another child!" His laughter stopped as suddenly as it had begun, and when he next spoke his voice was gruff, unforgiving in its tone. "Reminds me of Sarah. How is Sarah, by the way?"

"Our child, Sarah," said Eleanor, "is in boarding school." She was at pains to speak this very clearly. She wanted nothing misunderstood. "Sarah likes it fine."

Frank did not say that she ought to. He hoped he didn't need to remind Eleanor what it was costing him.

Eleanor relaxed, reaching over to pat Frank's arm. "You're a very young man," she advised him, soothingly. "You have a lot of time and I see no reason to rush into any permanent arrangement with your young lady friend." But Frank retained his gloom, thinking it necessary that Eleanor be made to recognize the air of their tainted partnership.

Gómez reappeared. He rattled the doorknob and called to Madeline and instantly something crashed against the other side of the door. Gómez didn't appear to mind. Again he threaded through the room, remarking to this or that empty chair: "The Mademoiselle would like perhaps the tour? The Mademoiselle is occupied?" He begged a chair's pardon—*"Muy bien—y usted?"*—and sat in one. The simple explanation occurred to Eleanor: it was the tourists and not his own twisted longings that had driven Gómez crazy—the tourists and the *inmigrante norteamericanos* who forced him each day into his cruel white suit.

"The Mademoiselles are desiring company, yes? The Mademoiselles—how to say it—are lost? *Perdido? Qué pasa*, lovely Mademoiselle. He went on talking to the empty tables in his usual way. Presently, perhaps, Madeline would come out and sit with him.

Frank was twitching. It seemed unjust, his having to put up with Eleanor's childishness and Gómez as well. Eleanor was batting flies from her face, routinely, as if entranced, and the flies did not appear to object. Frank followed her stare and saw nothing to deserve such scrutiny: a collapsed section of plaza wall and above it the mouth of Calle de la Noche de la mil Lunas. Her look was totally vacant and the enormity contained in such a look never failed to distress him. In this instance, watching her, it seemed to contain by its very absence so much of his life with her, a life that in retrospect seemed hardly to

116

have been his own. He was getting too old for this, had never been comfortable in the presence of a woman he couldn't desire. It amazed him, now that he thought of it, that he could no longer remember what it had been like to sleep with her, quite forgetting that this had been the first memory to fall. And Sarah, too. A moment ago he had struggled to recall her name.

Eleanor continued her mindless brushing away of flies. Their own patterns of flight seemed undisturbed. He felt angry with himself—and reasonably so, he decided, for it had been absurd of him to agree to come here and sit with her these mornings to watch this asinine parade of mourners, this senseless passage of the El Flores dead.

He grasped her rebozo and tugged. "What is it, Eleanor?"

"I was shooing away flies," she said.

The mouth of the Street of Moons was suddenly filled. A black wedge, a shield, ten or twelve men and women abreast, with heads and shoulders that kept replacing their own—a black curtain of mourners just suddenly there. Mammoth black body now unfolding up the other side of the Plaza Principal.

"I was shooing away flies," said Eleanor, "and you know how that is. You see them but you don't." She was speaking in a hush, although she showed a certain excitement now. The mourners had begun their song; their dirge was halting and uneven, without harmony or even melody and a dirge only because it was slow. "I was shooing away flies," said Eleanor, "without seeing them, and suddenly there they were all coming at me, all the mourners, and for a moment I saw them all as flies, upright but still flies, all silently winging toward me, the men with their patched black suits and the women with their black rebozos and black lace and black veils."

"And then they turned," sighed Frank, "and headed for the church."

117

"So here it is," said Eleanor, "the bleak wedding of all our murdered souls."

Gómez left his table and came up to take a quiet chair at theirs. Madeline would presently come out and sit with them.

They had been viewing this same spectacle every morning for six days now.

"Look at him," said Frank. "The only man in town who before the flood already had a proper suit." He was speaking of the priest, Father García, who stood alone on the cathedral steps waiting for the dead to come to him. He was wrong of course. Here even the poorest family had its mourning clothes; they were passed down from generation to generation for there would not be a generation that did not have a need for them.

They could see—behind the glass walls, behind the black wrought-iron frames above the carriage wheels—the new wooden boxes holding the dead.

"Now I understand it," murmured Eleanor. "El Flores is where you come when you die. It's where they're sending the people this year."

Gómez chuckled and kissed her hand. The tie on his white shirt was white and Eleanor noticed now that he even wore a white polish on his nails. "The Mademoiselle is perhaps upset? The Mademoiselle would perhaps like a pill?"

She retrieved her hand and raised it to shield her eyes.

"Don't let me see it," she said, "whatever it is."

"See what?" Frank asked.

"Whatever it is."

She could see across the plaza one of Father García's attendants dusting and arranging his full black gown.

Gómez rose and returned to his former chair. Madeline appeared now out of the small office and stood by the door, though she wasn't looking at any of them, nor at the procession either. She stood with her legs apart, pressing a hand against her stomach, sweat beading her brow, a look of panic in her eyes.

Eleanor saw her but did not think to interfere. "They let them into El Flores," she was telling Frank, "but they allow no-one to leave for fear they'll spread what is so catching here. The señor and you and me and Maya with his art of the see-through dead and probably your cool Indian as well. What is it, Frank, that the spit-and-polish paratroopers say? The buck stops here."

Past the coffin mounts, over the kneeling figures at the head of the procession now at halt in front of the cathedral, she had a clear view of Father García high on the steps, his jewelled staff raised in benediction, his other grasping the shining silver cross and sweeping to embrace all who might be so contained—intoning over these dead and the vast previous dead whose spirits had now passed on into heaven—and all the time heedless, it would seem, of the sobbing women at his feet with tumefied and unctuous kisses for his perfectly arranged gown.

She saw above and to her left, walking the high flat roof of the Banco Nacional, a thin Mexican in a tight business suit with field glasses over his nose and trained on the field of mourners below. His sight was settling on this one, on that one, and passing on to another, and not until she saw the glitter of the lens in the sun did she again address Frank.

"I'm Pisces," she said. "A Pisces, as you may know, is insecure and unreliable. A Pisces is as apt to go to pieces in public as she is to fall asleep while a lover is kissing her hand." Her voice was high and perilous but secured by nothing she could account for. "That's what they tell me about what a Pisces is when they share my birth date and hour. The chart doesn't lie but the birthday can. Do you believe that, Frank? Am I unreliable and insecure? Actually, I'm quite the opposite. I'm so secure in my breakdown that it frightens me. I'm like the ice skater must feel when he's at the bottom of the pond."

She looked over at the roof of the Banco Nacional and observed that the field glasses were still fixed on her table.

"Do you know that statue of Morelos in Janitzio in the middle of the lake? It's so high a person can't climb it. Do you remember Nüno de Guzman, the avaricious conquistador? They say he liked to roast people alive, especially local Tarascan chiefs who refused his commands. There are murals painted inside the statue of Morelos and in panel after panel the artist is roasting Nüno de Guzman, avaricious conquistador. Does it do any good? Is his roasting too late? Anyway, I once climbed up Morelos, for that was always a thing I vowed one day I'd do. Not climb Morelos—whose statue I didn't know about—but stand up straight inside the skull of a man who had been emptied of everything he might ever have had —for that's what statues are. Standing up in Morelos was the next best thing to standing up inside you. But do you know? I got dizzy, I couldn't even take my hands from my eyes to look at the view. Don't let me see it, I said, whatever it is! The Morelos ticket taker was waiting at the foot of the stairs when I came down. I asked him if anyone ever fell. 'Fall?' he said. 'That isn't necessary, as no-one climbs.' Do you suppose I dreamed it, Frank? Have I still never found myself in a position to look out through the eyes of a man? Not through Morelos' and never through yours because I've never been cool Indian enough. Actually I'm not Pisces, but if I am, I'm a Pisces who isn't sure. Not Pisces and I'm not 28 or 30 years old, I'm more in the vicinity of 405. Look at me, Frank. Have I aged? I'm 800 now and, like Methuselah, I've outlived all my wives. Now I'm 5010. In another second I'll be 28,000 and if I don't slow down soon I'll be older than all the dead out there. That's what it means being a Pisces. You can never catch up with yourself because you're always in a race with something else that doesn't slow down. Maybe I'm trying to catch up with the

cool Indian I once thought I was and which I continued to believe I was until the morning last winter when I waked up and
discovered that the body I had been sleeping beside was my
own, that the person I was bedding with was me. Where were
you Frank?—all those years?"

Frank did not trust himself to reply. He felt uneasy and
sullen and even sinned against. It was unkind and unfair and
against the rules for Eleanor to unburden herself of all this.
He had agreed to come here and sit with her and review this
ridiculous passing of the dead but he had not come here to
listen to Eleanor's fanciful insults and obscure accusations.
Yes, yes, it was perhaps true and she had cause. No doubt she
did feel her youth was behind her, that it had somehow been
violated, but how could she blame him for that? Doubtless her
dissatisfactions were real, they might even be urgent, he didn't
question that she sometimes suffered, but she had no right to
blame him for her own failures.

Yet he could remember now certain strange mornings when
he waked in bed beside her, the two of them silent and staring
at the ceiling, at the walls, the sun streaming through their
window and each of them listening for the low groan of life
that was elsewhere—that was always elsewhere, *anywhere*,
never there in that room and in that bed they shared. They had
never liked each other or respected or trusted each other—
perhaps that much was true—but they were married and he
knew—he would insist on this—that he had given it his best.

The man on the roof of the Banco Nacional was no longer
in sight. The first glass coffin mount was moving on ahead,
another was moving into place. The dirge the mourners sang
rose in volume, waiting for the priest's flash of jewels to die
down again. Their march was less orderly now, an inelegant
straggling face—without the cohesion of purpose now that the
first dead had been blessed, now that the ritual had prepared
his body for its escape from earth—now that only the cemetery

lay ahead.

The priest raised his arms over the second entrapped soul and the women rushed up to kiss his gown.

The procession passed slowly in front of the Bodega. Eleanor could see the women eyeing their table through their veils. The march would circle the plaza and wind up Calle de San Francisco and eventually empty into the *cementario* high above the village where the lake could not get to it. Then some of them would reassemble at the *funeraría* on Calle de la Noche de la mil Lunas and others would join them and the death procession would begin all over again.

Frank stamped out his cigarette on the red tile floor.

Gómez quit his table and went into the Bodega kitchen, reappearing a few minutes later with a cup of hot coffee which he took in to Madeline.

Eleanor could hear Madeline's harsh voice lifting in resentful gratitude even as she watched the mourners filing by. The dead, in their coffins behind the polished windows, had surely never known such comfort when alive. They rode over life now, a due and proper reward. A dog ran in a bewildered way along the outer column of marchers and someone kicked him spinning over the stones. The dog crawled on his stomach, debated a moment, and trotted awkwardly back to sniff once more at the mourners' heels. Those at the procession's rear were being urged along by one of the health inspectors but it was the priest, of course, who determined the pace and he seemed to be in no hurry. The business of God could not be rushed by the inspector from Morelia with his talk of plague and pestilence, for the inspector from Morelia was a stranger here and unused to the pace of life in El Flores. Let him post his notices and place his guards around the baneful waters of the lake and around those pernicious fountains in the village but there the responsibility of the inspector from Morelia ended.

How many now? It was bad luck to count the dead and Eleanor believed in bad luck, but in five days now she had counted enough to keep her bad luck running for some time to come; no, it would not do to change her luck now.

The roof of the Banco Nacional was still empty. Only the mossy configuration of madonnas carved in relief against the stone was looking at her.

Madeline was crying aloud inside Gómez' office. She was pleading with the Mexican but what she wanted exactly Eleanor couldn't say.

The worst was over. Everyone was saying the worst was over; indeed, they had been saying it from the start. Soon the heavy tourist buses of Tres Estrellas de Oro would roar around the plaza corner, the *mercado* peddlers would appear, the Posado de Don Vasco would fill, La Chica would open its doors and the Alameda whose *pescado blanco* was quite acceptable. The coffin mounts would be returned to Morelia and eventually, all in good time—*mañana, por cierto mañana!*—the workmen or the rain or more likely a combination of both would clear the rubble and scent of death in El Flores.

"For heaven's sakes," complained Frank, "why does she continue to put up with that man?"

Eleanor felt no compassion for Madeline with her desperate tears. They were urgent, but ask her and she would not know herself why she was crying and Eleanor could not tell her. Gómez could not tell her either and Frank could only ask her to shut up.

"Oh, look!" exclaimed Frank, "here comes Nora Meyer Jones!" He rose quickly, waving to the girl striding gracefully toward them down the Street of Moons.

"Sit down, Frank," Eleanor instructed him. He stared at her out of curiosity, but then did sit down. Eleanor meant nothing by this. She simply preferred that Nora Meyer Jones be left free to find her own way to them—to them or to someone else

123

or some other place. It was this, the accidental design, that gave pattern to a life.

The mourners hid her away. Eleanor grasped Frank's arm, as much as to say, Frank I want your attention now. She had a glimpse of binoculars above the banco wall.

"Frank," she said, "the time from exposure to illness to death is all within a period of 36 hours. The illness results from one or a combination of any of the three known means of exposure. First, you may be exposed through the food you eat. Second, through the water you drink and third, through contact with anyone who has been exposed to the previous two."

"Oh, Christ," moaned Frank, "Eleanor, can't you sit still?"

"This is the way it works. You feel a little worse each day, you run a fever, the fever rises, you suffer alternating or at times concurrent chills. You sweat horribly. You get headaches, you get diarrhea. Finally, all the vast and perpetual body pains accumulate and force you into a kind of drowsy stupor and your senses gradually wear thin. You waste away, you're able to watch your own death taking place and finlly when it happens you're ready to welcome it, you go peacefully as the clouds on a sweet summer day because there's nothing to stop you anymore. It's the way I felt last winter when I waked beside you and you said you were leaving me. Frank, how do you feel?"

"I feel fine," replied Frank, "though I thank you for all the information."

The bells in the three steeples at the head of the plaza struck and he listened to the tolls, wondering whether the bell ringer would this time confuse his count. He looked over the heads of the mourners for sight of Nora Meyer Jones but she was evidently hidden away somewhere within their maze.

"The Saint is loco, the Saint is terrible. Death here is all leisure, Frank. You can walk up San Antonio at your leisure

or make love to Nora Meyer Jones if that's your pleasure. But
no matter how extended it is it finally has to empty into something else, if only into more leisure. This breakfast has been
at our leisure, a slow leisure on its way to becoming our own
version of the El Flores death."

Frank lit another cigarette and stood, smiling down on her.
"Speak for yourself, Eleanor." The bells on San Antonio
pealed, replying quickly this time to those in the plaza. The
last coffin was being blessed. Very soon now the plaza would
be empty and they would see the mourners gathered at the
cementerio. Already the diggers were up there waiting, trapped
in their own penthouse ritual above the *posada's* roof.

Meanwhile, on the roof of the Banco Nacional, the painter
Maya was now in clear view. He had erected his easel, he had
his sketch pad and pencils, his oils, his binoculars too.

Nora Meyer Jones stood by the fountain at the plaza's
centre, pointing to him. "Look! The ghoul! The ghoul!"

Abruptly she wheeled and charged across the street toward
them, weaving through the mourners—entering the Bodega
now in a splash of enthusiasm. "God!" she cried—"God, I
hate waking alone, it's like waking on an island by yourself!"
She advanced on Eleanor, holding out her hand. "Are you *it*?
Are you the wife? I thought he was lying! Hello, my name is
Nora Meyer Jones. You can call me one but don't call me all!"
She took Eleanor's hand and shook it hard. She had bright,
beautiful eyes and could not get all her smile into them. She
straddled the chair, quickly rose again. "Who's crying? Is
someone crying? What's going on here?" She strode across the
floor, yanked open the office door. "Hi!" she said, "what's the
trouble here?" Madeline raised a startled head; Gómez turned
slowly in his chair. "Are you the waiter?" she said to him. "Can
I get some food around here? I'm starved! Plumb famished
through to bone."

She didn't wait for an answer. She came quickly back to

their table and draped her arms around Frank. "You don't mind?" she asked Eleanor. "Good! I've always been nuts for older men!"

Frank blinked good will at Eleanor. Eleanor blinked it back at him. The dirge ended in the plaza. The mourners advanced on up the hill. Up on the bank's roof, with extended arm, thumb uplifted, Maya was sighting down on their table. Eleanor sat erect, her expression beatific, hands laced across her bosom as if she held there the scarlet rose which only herself and Maya and Death's Angel could see and enjoy.

For Love of Gómez

The bells in the three steeples in the plaza cathedral were first to announce the midday hour and a minute or so later the rather timid bells from the poor church of San Antonio on the hillside pealed their thin acknowledgment; very soon afterward, as had become their custom, Sr. Gómez and his American companion Madeline appeared noisily out of the side wooden door so long weighted by its many black iron bolts and wide encrusted bars—to which Gómez had recently added the black metal crucifix which Madeline, among others, found so obscene—and made their way in unforgiving silence over the beautiful grass to the three lawn chairs which Don José and Manuel had today at the señor's instructions situated in a shadeless area some little distance up from the pool.

Madeline was brooding, which was not unusual, moving along sluggishly and with an intentionally unpleasant whine, her head down, now and again summoning sufficient energy to enable her to cast a malevolent glance over the spacious grounds, past the two Mexicans working in shoddy disgrace at the pool, and over the elegant Gómez who now was hastening on in front of her either to evade for a moment the girl's harsh noises or to arrange the glass lawn table between their chairs with the precise symmetry he required for these occasions.

Approaching distantly behind them was the señor's loyal dona, Señora Pesuna—carrying their noon provisions close to her stomach and with the fixed attention of both hands, in the first place because she much admired the artistry of the silver tray on which their refreshment rode, and in the second place because she could well remember spilling, some three weeks ago, a full pitcher of sangria over the demented girl's dress. True, it had not been her fault, as the señor had elaborately insisted, but it had since been the dona's intention to avoid the skinny and implacable *gringita* whenever possible.

The dona arrived at the chairs in time to hear the American girl's shrill voice complaining about something, about the sun perhaps, for she was flinging emaciated arms up to the sky much as if God Himself had somehow offended her in the creation of this beautiful day. The dona emptied her tray promptly, responding with a grunt to the señor's kind expressions of gratitude—wanting to hurry back to the safety of the señor's grand casa, for she had a fear of what she might see today in the crooked eyes of the señor's moody guest. She was herself without luck, burdened by the unfortunate hoof of the bull—each of her three husbands had died—but the impossible señorita was truly damned, *maldita*, for she had at once the eyes of the cow still nursing and those of the angry bull in a rage to kill.

As it happened, however, Madeline immediately calmed down, turning to them a pointedly bemused expression that seemed to be saying, "You see, I do have control, nothing you may do to me today shall affect me!"—thus accepting with uncharacteristic grace the gay multicoloured chair which the señor, by the sweeping of his hand, indicated might serve her needs this afternoon. She unfolded the chair to its full length and reclined in it without additional ceremony, accepting too the tall beautiful drink in the embossed silver glass which

Gómez now had poured for her. "Thank you," she said civilly, in a voice even approaching happiness, and the señor responded with "*De nada,*" it is nothing, his voice low, only the faintest amusement showing in his eyes.

The girl stretched out languidly under the sun, and the señor also leaned back, clearly relaxing, pulling his wide-brimmed hat down low over his brow until the sun was obscured. She was in her bathing suit as was customary at this hour, and Sr. Gómez wore his usual white ensemble: the perfectly tailored white suit, his high brushed-suede boots and the magnificent sombrero. She tasted and had no immediate complaint against the sangria which the señor today had especially prepared for her; for himself his dona had brought a bottle of Santo Thomas wine, the San Emilion label—and he too tasted his drink and declared it palatable, though somewhat to his surprise, for this native wine had never been a favourite.

"The Mademoiselle," he inquired, "is she comfortable?"

"I'm just peachy," the girl replied; and while this expression was familiar and offensive to the trained ear of Sr. Gómez, it was delivered without the girl's usual insistence of acrimonious wit, and so the señor was content for the moment to smile agreeably and pat her warm knee.

The sun droned overhead and for half an hour neither had much more to say. Manuel and the elderly Don José looked up from time to time from their work at the pool to reassure themselves of this fact and to renew their individual wagers as to how long this unexpected situation might continue— while Señora Pesuna paused occasionally at the window in the kitchen where their *comida* was being prepared, there to issue another of her muttered and tainted prayers to the Virgin. The dona's prayer, however, concerned neither the wickedness of Sr. Gómez nor that of his mistress, but was meant solely for the relief of her third husband whose life the recent pestilence of the lake had claimed.

The sun thickened; it expanded and seemed to hang ever nearer; it poured down in waves, hugged the señor's beautiful garden, came weighted and as if spooned into the air in ripples; more and more Madeline began to shift and groan in her chair. Her sight turned longingly toward the pool, and she raked spiteful glances at the señor sitting so composedly, so blissfully, close by.

"The Mademoiselle," the señor said, smiling lazily, "—she finds the sun too hot? It is—how to say it?—*la sartén*, the frying pan?"

Despite her intentions, Madeline could not resist this clear invitation to tell Gómez what he could do with himself. "You," she muttered bitterly, pausing to wipe damp hair from her face, "can go to hell!" The señor smiled and nodded his head idiotically as if he were one in a pair singing harmony. "Damn you and your stupid swimming pool," declared Madeline. "You do it this way only to spite me. You can't stand the idea that I might ever enjoy myself."

The señor laughed, which further irritated her, though she fully understood this to be his intention. "But I don't care," she concluded, her voice lifting to the high nasal pitch that the señor and all who were acquainted with her so much deplored —"Nothing you do can bother me!" Sighing now, satisfied that her integrity remained intact, Madeline rolled her back to the sun, drawing up a slow arm across her enervated and sweating face so that her eyes might be shielded.

The señor casually lit up his filtered Delicado, and let his gaze float blithely about.

"Once more," he said softly, "I will explain to the Mademoiselle, for I know she has not been herself lately and finds our customs unfamiliar. Today we must drain the pool—"

"With buckets!" interrupted Madeline, who could not help herself.

"Then the pool must dry. Afterward, we must whitewash

the pool and then again it must dry. With these necessities successfully concluded. Don José will attach the garden hose and the swimming pool will begin to fill."

"It's outrageous!" shrieked the girl.

The señor said no more until her contortions had subsided. Then he lifted his left hand and slowly counted off the days on his fingers: "Once more I will explain. Three days to empty this pool. One to dry. Another to whitewash the floor and walls. Perhaps two for this whitewash to dry. Three addittional days for the hose to fill."

"Yeah!" said the girl. "With your little half-inch hose. I could spit and fill it up quicker."

"At that point," continued the señor, "the Mademoiselle may have her swim."

"Screw it," whispered Madeline.

"So," said the señor. "Ten days, less or more. Who is to say? But ten, I should think. Though we cannot be certain. My men have many other jobs to perform. They may tire of this business with the swimming pool. They do not understand the Mademoiselle's urgency, you see." He shrugged, extending his arms to full-length. *"Por que no?"* Why not?

He blew cigarette smoke toward the girl, and laughed contentedly. He liked to think that he differed from his countrymen in that he measured time by the future rather than the past; it was this trait, he believed, that had ennabled him to tolerate this vain and belligerent and altogether ludicrous girl for so long.

Madeline had turned away. She was not, in fact, listening. She had already thought this matter through, and was in no mood for his mocking explanations: she wanted to swim; she could not; someone, therefore, was to blame. She stared across the lawn at the tasteless crucifix mounted on his door, and kicked irritably at the flies, at the very air. Soon. A few more hours. Then she would be going home. Purging all reminders of her humiliation here: this miserable Mexico with its ignorant cacophony of misery and guile and neglect—of this drab wrecked village with its endless and blissful acceptance of everything from natural physical disasters—wind, fire, flood and plague—to the meanest and most crucial of personal deprivations. A stagnant, blistering place that lacked even the saving grace of what one might term a higher tragedy because it was throughout base and impotent—and surviving only because tourists such as herself came and spent their money here.

"Qué pasa?" the señor asked. What is the matter? He rubbed his hands together, winking. *"Fuma usted?"* Perhaps the enchanted Mademoiselle would like the cigarette?

Madeline, regarding him coldly, did not reply. She thought: Smoke, by all means. Never mind my feelings, what could my feelings or wishes possibly matter? His long fingers, extended, secured the cigarette elegantly, his teeth closed on the oval shape, and her own cheeks sucked in as he pulled in the smoke. Loathsome! she thought. God, I hate this man!

She hurled herself flat against the chair's webbing, again yanked the clinging hair from her face. . . and found herself staring in sudden fury at the thick shaded grass beneath the vacant third chair. Nowhere else in El Flores was there a lawn so luxuriously verdant and thriving. Throughout the village the earth was parched and decaying, all dry stubble, putrid debris all over. She was convinced that Gómez went to such extremes in the care of his garden not out of any pride or love of grass but simply to deny her the one pleasure available to her here. The pool! she thought. His goddamn pool! He is happy only when I suffer!

A whine escaped her briefly and she thrashed against her chair's scratchy webbing. Sticky! Everything so God-awful primitive and depressing! She rolled on her back, lifted herself, and stared with consuming hatred at the two men working at the pool. Look at them! she thought. Those disgusting idiots! Those fools. Bailing out that huge pool with their two yellow leaky buckets! God, they're insane! It will take weeks!

One of them, young Manuel, down on his knees at the pool's edge, saw her looking and grinned his toothless grin, jabbing a dark finger at his dripping bucket.

She took up her glass from the table and drank to its bottom. Gómez was watching her, but she didn't care. She would endure him these last hours. She would not let him upset her. Today, she thought, I'm in the driver's seat. She would tell him, before it was over, what a monkey she thought him to be. She lay back down, groaning. She would have to pack soon. Too bad she had put it off. But she couldn't have anyway, or Gómez would have noticed. Let him remain ignorant, she thought. When I go it will blow him out of the park. She wondered about the dona. Had that lazy bitch washed her clothes? Were they ironed? Gómez, she thought, lets that woman get away with too much. She steals. I'll tell on her before I go. Last week she returned my new shirt with all the buttons gone. Every one.

But they all steal, she thought. She would tell them all off before she left: Gómez and his dona and that trash down at the pool. She hated them all. Ignorant, filthy, shiftless—she rolled over and reached for her glass—*foreigners*, she had almost said. But she was the foreigner. She was in their grimy country and at their mercy. Dependent on their sickening, toadish hospitality. Had to put up with their imbecilic grins and that stupid green shit in her eggs. Had been forced to put up with *him!*

She stared at the señor, squinting; her mouth screwed into a grimace, and she found herself speaking:

"Tell that fat cow of yours to bring me more sangria!"

The señor said nothing. He did not even look her way.

In a little while she lay back down, stunned and depleted by the heat, in agony from the unrelenting monotony of this dull hour. "Now," she said, her voice slurring. "This very minute! I'm thirsty! It must be 100 degrees out here."

"*Desde luego,*" she heard him reply cheerfully—of course —and knew that he would be beckoning to the two idiots labouring so ridiculously at the pool, one of whom would presently appear and be sent to the casa where he would tell the slovenly dona that the señor desired another pitcher for his señorita.

Again her sight took in the vacant chair and it occurred to her to wonder if Gómez was expecting anyone. Well, no matter. She would have a use for it if he didn't.

She closed her eyes, and waited. The sun was insufferable, they were all pigs, this country was an unholy terror, but she could abide it—or so her thoughts went—this last day.

So here they are. Since noon they have been reclining in gay lawn chairs out under the sun in the señor's large beautiful garden, Madeline in her bathing suit, the señor in his impeccable white suit, boots and sombrero. The dona arrives to replenish the sangria and the señor informs her pleasantly that they will be having their *comida* here at these chairs under the sun. Señora Pesuna recognizes this as madness but reflects on it not at all; it is not her duty to suggest alternatives to the señor. Old Don José and Manuel quit their labour at the pool and disappear briefly into deep shade to drink Coco-Cola and chew on crusty *bolillos* in advance of lunch, for though they are hungry it would be impolite of them to dine fully before the señor has been served his. The señor, as if transfixed, stares at the pool and over these lovely grounds which the recent flood has fortunately spared. His view embraces his fine stand of trees—pecan and orange and avocado—which his grandfather had planted and through which is visible now the shore end of Calle de la Noche de la mil Lunas and the placid blue of the lake. Occasionally he will remove his sombrero and fan his dark handsome face which has dampened not at all in this high sun. He smiles, and also waits. Madeline dozes. The señor will periodically turn and regard her perspiring face almost with tenderness. He bends forward sometimes and brushes flies from her legs that glisten under heavy applications of coconut oil. The air here is thick with its smell. Don José and Manuel resume their duties at the pool. The señor sips at the Santo Thomas wine. In one hour its volume has dropped scarcely a thimbleful.

They have been together eight weeks now.

The señor smokes and the smoke wraps overhead in the windless air; all of El Flores, all of Mexico, seems to have connived with them in the making of this sultry hour. From where he sits the pool shows a surface of green scum. The speed with which the algae overtake this body of water never fails to amuse and intrigue Sr. Gómez. For weeks—for two or three—it will stand—clear, lovely, unspoiled—but within a few hours after the first patch forms, the pool's entire surface will surrender to this slime. No, this speed the señor does not understand. But although he can not accustom himself to it, he is on the whole not displeased. Such is the way of nature and he will deal with it in his customary way: he will empty the pool, feed the scum back into the earth, and his garden will prosper. His companion may shake her pathetic fists and screech, she may further degrade herself with these innumerable insults and accusations—but such behaviour too presents no special problem. This also is the way of nature. These stubborn Mademoiselles must be dealt with as his pool is. They must first be emptied—humiliated—and then they may be filled.

Madeline was stirring. Again he filled her glass, placing it at the table's edge where she might reach it without struggling. He consulted his watch, nodded, and contemplated the empty chair. His pleasure in arranging this chair for the use of the Mademoiselle's father was considerable. It would remain vacant—at any rate it would never be occupied by the señor from across the border—and Gómez regretted this somewhat for he admitted to a mild curiosity about the sort of parent who could sire someone of Madeline's selfish, venal, and deluded nature. He had not enjoyed these eight weeks, but his time with the truculent Mademoiselle had fortified him in his views. His actions with regard to her and her predecessors were perhaps questionable on some abstract level, but he was now more than ever confident that his methods were both necessary and deserved.

Madeline waked, grumbling, and reached for her drink.

In Mexico, it seemed to the señor, the norteamericanos were constantly so reaching.

She brought the glass down, took several deep breaths, then swallowed the remainder in her glass.

The señor promptly refilled the tall container, and watched the girl rub her eyes in petulant drowsiness. With her knuckles, like a child. He smiled compassionately. She was of course unappreciative of his foresight in lacing this mixture with a quantity of Oso Negro Ginebra sufficient to propel her ahead of time into her afternoon siesta. No. The unruly Mademoiselle would not know that she had been drunk since ten minutes after spreading herself so possessively into his chair.

"Where's your lackey?" she now demanded.

He raised a curious brow, finding the word unfamiliar.

"Your donkey," she said. "Your slovenly dona. Where's our lunch, or whatever you call it?" The señor blinked consolingly, and she blinked back. "What time is it?" she asked, screwing up her eyes at the sun. "God, I'm about dead. I don't see how you can *breathe* in all those clothes."

Gómez turned to her the patronizing smile she found so exasperating. He did not trouble himself to inform her that

136

in his view there was very little the infirmed and irrational and atrociously impaired Mademoiselle from the USA did understand. Once more he noted that whenever the girl became sullen her eyes crossed ever so slightly. He found himself pondering whether this was a trait shared by norteamericana women.

"This is not as sweet as the first pitcher," the girl complained, indicating the sangria. "I don't like it."

The señor refrained from observing aloud that she had been consuming the liquid with what appeared considerable thirst.

She fell exhausted back into the chair.

Her bikini top—a Casa Rosa creation from the señor's own shop—had stretched, leaving one breast now fully exposed. Gómez shifted in his chair to avoid this unnecessary distraction. She scratched irritably at one uplifted knee, and wiped the oil residue from her nails by stabbing her hand repeatedly into the grass. She winked at his sour face. Buster, she thought, you think I have a contemptuous nature, but you haven't seen the half of it yet. Just wait till my Dad gets here.

The thought delighted her and for a moment she was mindless even of the heat. Her father was coming; he was coming this afternoon. He would fly down, was in the air this very minute; he would take her out of this pigsty called Mexico. Perhaps then this nasty man in his vile white suit would not be so cruel and smug and indifferent to her needs.

A finger poked into her rump. She turned her head to find him grinning at her. "Ah! The Mademoiselle has secrets, no? The Mademoiselle has the little bird?"

She frowned, moving away from his touch. What was he getting at? Did he suspect? I'm telling you nothing, she determined. Nothing!—and gained a moment's pleasure from this practice—as she thought of it—of uncharacteristic guile.

"You can't keep me here, you know," she said, taunting. "I can leave anytime I like. I'm not your cringing little nubile

137

white slave."

The señor pulled the white sombrero down over his brow. He slid deeper into the chair and placed one boot heel-to-toe over the other. They were beautifully-made boots and he treasured them greatly.

"You'll see," said Madeline, enjoying herself. "I'll walk out on you and you won't be so preachy and superior then!"

Gómez had no interest in this. He found the girl's declarations trite and pathetic. He rose, and flicked a spot of ash from his suitcoat—stared off into the trees for a moment, and then sat back down, sighing, lifting his face to meet the sun. He was enamoured of this house, of these grounds, and was capable —such times as this—of believing the sun existed solely for him.

"I might!" Madeline said. "I might not even be here tomorrow!"

With this remark her voice lost much of its control. It carried, high and brittle, to the two Mexicans working at the pool. They held their buckets by their sides and their attention lingered on her as if they believed that by sight alone they could explain the baffling presence of this naked *gringita* with the skinny voice and *la grande boca*, the big mouth, and the crazy love for the unpleasant swimming pool.

The señor spoke with his eyes closed, his hands laced over his chest. "The Mademoiselle has acquired confidence. I congratulate the Mademoiselle. Perhaps the Mademoiselle has received news?"

Madeline had been swatting flies. She turned quickly and gave his face a confused search. "What do you mean, news? What are you talking about?"

He waved a slender hand, disarmingly. His expression was untroubled and adoringly innocent. He tipped himself forward, helpfully, and whispered: "The Mademoiselle has perhaps engaged the services of the *teléfono*? The financial affairs of the Mademoiselle are perhaps soon to be in order?" He relaxed back into his chair, radiant. *"Qué bonito!"* How nice.

Madeline felt herself swept along by a tide of familiar resentment. She retreated into thoughtful silence. She had no way of knowing that the señor had arrangements with the señorita at the telephone office whose services Madeline had yesterday engaged; that he was in daily communication with agreeable unshaven Filipe at the telegraph office where she had for so long been expecting money; nor that the untidy employees at La Casa de Correos routinely reported—and frequently sent on ahead for his perusal—to him on the contents of apartamento 29, her private and secret letter box.

The sky remained absolutely clear, and the sun seemed larger and nearer, like a giant living thing lured by the need for human company. On the street outside the señor's walls an *helados* vendor could be heard rattling his cart over the stones, crying with a cadence.

Madeline dipped her fingers into the pitcher, searching for ice, but the ice had melted, so she smeared the cold liquid over her brow and throat. "Americans," she exclaimed suddenly, "should not be allowed into this stupid country!" She felt a renewed surge of contempt—of utter hatred for everything that moved before her eyes—and settled back again against the chair's webbing, calmed and enriched by the insight this attitude afforded her.

The assertion brought no change to the señor's features. Just now his interest was in the two workers down by the pool. Such foolish men—worthless!—yet they gave him much pleasure. He admitted to a certain pride in them. They were slow, they were witless—they in fact had not a single brain in their heads—but it pleased the señor to consider that he would not exchange one of them for ten... for a hundred... vapid *immigrantes* such as Madeline. They, after all, could work. But the Mademoiselle! What a waste! One longed to turn the skin on all of them, to shout *Márchese! Salga! Vaya!*—Leave! Go home!—and drive them across the border as the *leñadores* drives his burro past the watering-hole. *Por qué no?* Because they always came, alone and in pairs, by full car, boat, plane and train, with their full pocketbooks and forever crying Thief! Thief! I have been robbed! or crying out wherever one saw them, *Ne entiendo! No entiendo!* Speak the *inglés*! . . . or, like Madeline, abandoned though yet unweaned, stunted and purposeless and most often in tears, they came to his door begging, crying I am hungry, I am cold, I have no place to stay, no money, Oh señor what will I do? and always with the same explanation It is not my fault señor *no es culpa mía*, the fault is with your bank which will not honour my cheque, it is the fault of your post office which has lost my mail, with your water which is not pure and your food which has made me sick Oh señor *Socorro Socorro!* help me señor and I will do anything. . . but rarely remembering to say *gracias* and injured if they should be compelled to say *please*—for all that belonged to anyone else in this country was theirs anyway and in any case their money would soon arrive and they would be independent, they would be themselves once more, they would need no-one's filthy help.

The situation was desperate, Sr. Gómez reflected—whenever was it not?

He sipped at his wine, smiling at Madeline in sombre fascination, and in fact feeling something akin to a fondness for the deep worry lines in her brow and the narrow slitted eyes that could not see exactly straight. . . glancing away from her now and then to nod his head in acceptance of the attention of Don José and Manuel who stood with imbecilic grins in the scum-coated water at the shallow end of the pool, lifting their twin buckets and jabbing deliriously at the dripping sides so that he might better understand and appreciate the zealous intent with which they were applying themselves in reducing the level of water in the pool so that all might be happy once more.

"Dopes!" fumed Madeline. "Idiots! At home we'd shoot people like that."

"Ah,' said Gómez, "but if I shoot them we should have to do the work ourselves." His melodic voice chided her.

"God!" she cried, her teeth clenched. She sighted Manuel's glum pudgy wife, nineteen and looking 40, seated under one of the pecan trees, nursing her youngest child while her two small sons sat obediently beside her, staring across at them. "She's filthy," Madeline said, pointing to her. "Make her go away."

"On the contrary," said the señor, "I myself know she bathes once each week. Quite on the other hand the dirt is good for them. How otherwise will they build up an immunity against the germs?"

Madeline groaned in disgust. She was sick of talking to him. She was tired of this kind of nonsense and even feeling a nostalgic longing for her parents' house in Los Angeles and for the one or two intelligent friends she had run about with there. She sat up with a new fervour, turning and planting her feet in the grass, directly facing him.

"I want a cigarette," she said.

His chin showed a blue crescent of beard cut smoothly down to skin. His long black lashes curled. They were, in her view, disgusting on a man. For a time she had even believed them artificial. She clenched her fist, waiting, determined this time to have her cigarette, and at the same time thinking *soon, soon, in a few hours my father will be here.* But she didn't want to think now of her father who didn't trust her enough to merely send the money. No, he had to come down here himself and preach to her, tell her what an aggravation she was to him— and finally drag her home the way one would a child. As if she would stay in this stupid country one minute longer than necessary.

"But I sent you money before," he had told her yesterday on the phone. "What did you do with it?"

"That was Raymond," she had said. "Raymond spent it."

"Someone always does. You always have one excuse or another."

"He was no good, a pig, how was I supposed to know?"

"You never know," her father had said. "It's always punks that attract you."

She stared at the closed eyes of Sr. Gómez—at his nose, at his thin lips now purple in the sun—and recoiled at the faint stirrings of desire. It's disgusting, she thought—furious not at herself but at this reminder of all the men whose mouths had ever touched her. Of Raymond, for instance, with his petty moods and cheap tricks and lousy Spanish and the sneering belief that he was invincible. *You never know*, her father had said. Well, that was a lie. She knew all too soon: scum, pigs, each of them, not one worth wiping her shoes on.

She looked across the lawn at the two men bailing water from the pool. Impossibly ignorant, but at least they didn't have to suffer as she was suffering now. At least they could stand in that putrid water and stay cool. She felt unbearably hot and sweaty, and reached for the sangria. The ice had thinned the bitterness, it tasted delicious now. Sangria was a wonderful drink. You could sip it all afternoon and through the evening and when you finally went to bed, sleep—or whatever—was what you were ready for. And if you wakened the next day drowsy and stunned, what did it matter—because this was Mexico and Mexico was...

She felt dizzy, and put the pitcher down, wondering whether she was getting drunk. Surely a little wine couldn't... but no, it is the heat, she assured herself. Only the heat. In a civilized place there would be air conditioners but in El Flores even the street lights flickered and dimmed at night or the power went off altogether.

She swayed forward, touching her fingers to Gómez' cheek. Her fingers slid over his eyelids, his nose, touched lightly on his mouth. His expression did not change. You pig, she thought—but for the moment there was no vehemence in her mood. He was worse than Raymond, worse than her father— he was despicable and evil to the core—but his eccentricities were at least amusing. And he had money. His wardrobe was filled with white linen suits. The white boots he drooled over. His famous tinsel-sheeted front door. His stupid Café Bodega where no-one could eat without dying halfway through the meal. His beautiful garden with the crazy swimming pool that wasn't for swimming. . . . Malignant bastard. . . the sonofa-bitch. . . !

She lifted his hand and touched his fingers to her lips. "Gómez," she begged softly. "May I have a cigarette?"

His eyes opened and he shook his head.

"Please. . ." She reached for the package; he smacked her hand away. Her flesh stung, and tears came to her eyes. "But you promised me!" she said, her voice rising. "Yesterday you promised me I could smoke today!"

"What the señor gives he may take away," he said smoothly.

"I want a cigarette!" she cried, and wrenched at the pack— but again Gómez stung her hand. "The Mademoiselle is over-anxious," he murmured. "The Mademoiselle forgets herself."

She began shouting. "Let me have them! They are mine! You promised!" She caught his wrist and tried to tear them from his palm. Her body twisted and she tried to reach him with her teeth. "Give them to me! They're mine!"

"*Lo siento*, Mademoiselle," he whispered. Without warning his flat hand struck her across the face. "*Lo siento*." He smacked her again. "*Lo siento*." Again. I am sorry. I am sorry. *Perdone*, Mademoiselle. He kept on slapping her. She continued to kick and wriggle about, her neck snapping each time he struck.

Finally she stopped struggling. She did not attempt to dodge his blows. Her head was erect, she was smiling, inviting him to go on hitting her for as long as he wished.

Down at the pool the two workmen—and Manuel's wife and children under the tree—watched with tolerant unconcern, their faces masks of indifference, as though they were awaiting the coming of rain or flashes of lightning in a closing sky. *Por qué no?* Why not? Or so they thought. If these had come once they would come again later. If not soon, then soon after. If not then, then never. If never, then *tanto mejor*. So much the better.

"Ah," sighed the elderly Don José. *"El fumadores."* Is it the cigarettes?

"Sí-sí," replied Manuel. *"El vino."*

"Le grande amorio," murmured Don José, nodding.

To want the smoke, to have the wine, to be in love. *Bueno, bueno.* Nothing here ever changes. The coyote still runs through the señor's garden.

They laughed softly together and spoke with a sorrowful and polite indecision of *el blanco* señor and his *malnutrida gringita*—and after a few artless attempts to empty additional water from the pool they agreed it would be wise now while the señor was engaged to abandon their hard work for a good lunch and perhaps *más tarde*, later, a private moment or two in the shade, for this was good and exactly what two such hardworking men owed to themselves.

The señor was bad, *malísimo*, but only a little bad, for it was a man's duty to occasionally smack the face of his *puta*, for it was well understood that only a man's fist could keep the good whores gentle.

The señor was once more arranging the lawn chairs to their desired formation. Madeline was down on one knee in the grass, hacking for breath, and loudly sobbing. *"Cómo está usted?"* whispered the señor. "Sí, sí, have the cigarette, what am I thinking of? *Cómo quiero usted?* Of course you may have the cigarette. Have all the cigarettes." He crushed the mangled package into her hand. "Light up, have the smoke. By all means. The Mademoiselle will be herself again." He talked on in this way, grinning, quite calm himself, adamantly solicitous. She dropped the package and he replaced them into her unresisting hand. Her shoulders were now shaking a little less noticeably. She was on her knees crawling away from him. "Salud! To your health. The Mademoiselle is beautiful when she smokes. When she does not, the Mademoiselle she is *el toro de lidia,* the fighting bull." He lit one of his cigarettes, lifted her, and placed it between her lips. "Ah. Now the Mademoiselle is happy!"

Madeline was now whimpering. He gave her a shove away from the chairs. "Bravo. Let us take the little bull into the casa."

She stumbled ahead.

"I will advise the señora that our *comida* is to be delayed. Do you agree? Does the Mademoiselle find favour in this idea?"

Madeline whirled. "Don't touch me!" she screamed. "Don't you dare touch me!" Her fists were raised, and her red face contorted. "I'll kill you if you come near me!"

But she stood, waiting—with growing interest—and when the señor came abreast of her and wrapped his arm over her shoulder she walked along with him, meek, but not unwillingly, into the señor's casa and to his bed.

A short time later—after twenty minutes or so—the side wooden door again opened and the two made their way without incident to the waiting chairs. Madeline had retained her swim suit—indeed she had showered and seemed more than a little refreshed—while Sr. Gómez had exchanged his rumpled white suit for another identical to the first. With a courtly manner he now seated her. He held a flame to her cigarette, adjusted her head-rest, and encouraged her to lie down and relax in the sun in these few moments before the *comida* came.

She murmured her thanks in a faraway voice and the señor replied *"De nada"* and for some minutes kneeled beside her to spread the coconut oil over her skin.

He strolled down to the pool and there, stooping low, measured with a finger the water's descent from its original surface line. His workers had not yet returned and he saw no visible signs evidencing their existence in the adobe hut beyond the avocado trees. He looked up at the sky which was a cloudless lovely blue, consulted his watch, and reasoned with some certainty that he and Madeline would yet have time to eat before the coming of the afternoon rain. He loved this rain which arrived now each day and at about the same hour without fail, and found it unfathomable that the unpredictable Mademoiselle as a rule did not.

From her chair Madeline watched him stealthily. What had just happened in the señor's bedroom she had decided to ignore. She did not begrudge him these love-making acts—in this respect at least he was no more perverse than other men. And better, she conceded, than most. She poured coconut oil in the palm of her hand and rubbed the heavy liquid—Gómez would not allow her the purchase of a decent suntan oil—over her exposed stomach and shoulders and limbs. She smiled vacantly, her eyes wide, admiring the hard flatness of her stomach, the curve of her legs, the tight muscles of her thighs. Her full breasts, the smooth beauty of her skin.

Overhead, sputtering in slow flight, a single-engine plane appeared, flapping a message for the town. Madeline could not read the trailing banner, but she had seen the El Flores posters and correctly reasoned it to be advertising the bullfight in Morelia scheduled for the coming weekend. Dull grey in colour, cruising low, an antique. That, or junk, like all things here. The plane passed in front of the sun and momentarily disappeared; Madeline gasped and threw up her hands over her eyes, wounded by the sun's incredible glare. The plane knocked along miserably, and once more she looked up, hearing the flutter of the sign directly above her; the cloth was whipping about violently because the stupid pilot had not known enough to cut air holes into the thing.

The pilot was quite visible too and she could see him waving.

"Crash. . . I hope you do," she murmured aloud, and wrenched her arms behind her back to tighten the bikini strings. The friendliness of these people, as she had told Gómez more than once, she found personally nauseating. God knows what deceit it was intended to hide.

Gómez was not in sight. She had a moment of panic, thinking herself alone, but then she located his white figure near the wall at the street door which now was open. With him stood the El Flores padre, Father García, his black gown hanging wide at the ankles, his monk's cowl pushed back over his shoulder, his bald head shining in the sun. Both of them, like fools, looking up at the sky. Madeline turned away with a curse. Next to Gómez, the padre was the man she most despised in all of El Flores. Serving God, what a laugh that was! Since the day of the storm, after Raymond had taken her money and abandoned her here, her hatred for the priest and his church was without compromise. On that day, pelted by the rain and half out of her mind from the grief of Raymond's betrayal, she had battered on the cathedral door and implored the father to let her in—to help her—but he had refused. So if she were slut to Gómez now, the blame lay entirely with the church and that hypocrite.

I've been through hell, she thought, but everyone will have to admit that I never looked better.

It had crossed her mind that she ought to send colour postcards of herself to all the men she had ever known saying

Grieve, bastard, for all the good times you're missing now!

She looked back again at the door and saw Father García with his arm around Gómez' shoulder. Gómez was giving him money. Madeline flung herself back against the chair, her eyes closed, her fists shaking.

A few minutes later the plane again circled overhead, as if it had forgotten something on its first run; it hammered on away, taking its ragged message to another of the tiny villages hugging the lake.

The señor once more claimed his chair.

"I saw you," Madeline said, "giving a big wad of pesos to that monkey!"

The señor was obviously surprised at this outburst, but waited for her to continue.

"It may interest you to learn," said Madeline, "that yesterday I was seated on one of those benches in the plaza when your resident saint came up and sat beside me with that 'my child my child' routine of his."

The señor lifted a brow.

"He put his hand on me," she said. "He put his hand right here between my thighs."

This statement clearly disconcerted the señor. His hands fluttered hopelessly up and down, his view swept over the garden, went from tree to tree, before it came to rest again on Madeline's bent and glistening knees. Once or twice he started to speak but each time his hands fluttered up and whirled about and fell again with nothing spoken. It was not the Mademoiselle's story that aroused this discomfort. That the Mademoiselle was lying was assured. Did she go anywhere without first securing his permission? Did she speak to anyone without this being immediately reported to him? And did the Father not spend all of yesterday in Erongarequaro across the lake where some hint of the recent pestilence still remained? Had the Father not revealed as much a moment ago while requesting

148

money to aid those in Erongarequaro still infirmed? No, that the Mademoiselle had fabricated this ugly assertion the señor instantly perceived. But his hands lifted and fell, he searched the high branches of these trees, because he could not comprehend or even imagine why the Mademoiselle should be so compelled.

It did not occur to the señor—nor did Madeline admit to it —that she made this assertion merely because Gómez had given away money she had come to consider as partially and rightfully her own.

Señora Pesuna approached across the grass, bearing their *comida* on the beautiful silver tray earlier employed and which boasted now a large earthenware *olla* filled with a mixture that yet bubbled in its brown juices.

"What's this puke?" Madeline asked. But a second later she sniffed at the bowl and laughed as if to convey the notion that she had been joking—prompted to this move by the severity of the señor's expression and the realization that such rudeness was no longer necessary. This would very likely be her last meal at the señor's table, and she had no doubts that once she departed Gómez and his servants would richly regret her absence and be forced to admit that she was something other than the shallow, naïve American girl they had supposed her to be. They could go on thinking whatever they wished, however. She knew herself to be an altogether candid person, open and friendly and generous—and if she was ever considered anything less this was only because so few people really understood her or ever made an effort to get to know her.

"I give up," she said. "What is it?"

"*La sopa*," the dona replied. Soup. Only soup, señora. Soup, as anyone with eyes can see.

The bowl contained chicken giblets cooked with numerous unidentifiable vegetables over which floated, for good luck, scores of hot jalapeno chiles. Madeline tasted hers, frowning, and quickly reached for one of the two Tecate xxx beers the dona had provided. It was delicious, she told the woman, which was the case, and Señora Pesuna, no longer offended, hurried away to secure their second course, a fine pescado blanco taken from their own lake now that the health officials had declared the local fish free of contamination.

The señor dined lightly, in silence, with no apparent hunger. An inaccessible grief apeared to have overtaken him. He poured his beer into the lovely glass, and sat in jaded contemplation of the foam. He toyed with glass and bowl, clearly interested in neither. His fingers laced above his chest and now and then again his eyes rolled heavenward. It was Madeline, of course, who brought this on. The spirit of this woman would yield but it could not be broken. And yet what a curiously ignoble—what a marvellously vain and worthless—spirit it was. It withstood everything and in fact the more one attempted its mutilation the more it thrived. He could not accept Father García's timid boast that God was in every person, that the soul even of his volatile mistress resisted all such transgressions for the simple reason that the soul belongs alone to God. Foregoing the banality of such a claim, so the señor now asked himself, why should God continue to have an interest? No, not even the norteamericano God could be so long-suffering. The explanation, the señor concluded, lay entirely with her native origins. Only her native country could produce citizens of such interminable wretchedness and conceit, and in such numbers. Here in his country they might degrade themselves, they might behave with utter abandonment—secure in the knowledge that here it did not greatly matter. Their vanity still prevailed. They could be beasts but—*Están con los angeles*—their souls resided with the angels because they came from where they did. But inculcated how? By what? One could account for its prevalence neither by economics, their religion, nor by the racism always lurking in their blood. One could account for it not at all. *"No sé,"* muttered the señor. I don't know. Perhaps the issue was less complicated, after all. Perhaps it was to be explained by their diet, by the curious customs by which that diet was appeased: because they had so few reminders of the low order of life from whence they came.

"Perdone?" I'm sorry, what was it you said? He lifted his head; the Mademoiselle was speaking to him.

"I said," repeated Madeline, her voice thinning in a haughty cascade "—it wasn't the first time either!"

The señor, released from his doldrums, laughed heartily, enjoying the vision of Father García, whose sexual penchant was so well-known, with his hand on any woman's leg.

Madeline picked moodily at her fish. The fish had been steamed, and looked undercooked, which was why she didn't like steamed fish in the first place. "My father will pay you," she said.

The señor raised an interested, puzzled eye—

". . . for what you spent on me," Madeline said.

This too the señor thought very funny. He lifted his glass and toasted the thought.

"What's the matter with you?" asked Madeline. "You're nuts, you know. But you'll miss me when I'm gone."

The señor seemed to reflect on this. He poured another inch of cerveza from the Tecate can, ran his fingers under the lapels of his white suit—all the while appraising her across the table. "The señor," he said finally, "has been posing the question. The señor has been deciding what he must do with the poor Mademoiselle."

Madeline did not immediately take this in. Now that it had occurred to her, it seemed quite natural that Gómez should miss her. Raymond too had surprised her in this regard. Some weeks back she had received a brief letter from him, postmarked San Miguel de Allende and written in a grade-school scrawl, in which he had whined generally about the state of

151

his poverty and specifically about all the crude Americans there and which had ended with these hilarious words: *you were a BITCH Mady and I guess I LOVED you and MISS you and was a DOPE to cut out on you just because of worrying about where the old $ was coming from.*

The señor was again ignoring her. He soberly regarded the sky while one finger tapped repeatedly on his watch crystal, much as if he suposed he could predict the very minute the afternoon rain would commence falling.

Madeline twisted in her chair and clutched at his arm. "Listen," she said. "My father is coming. I am leaving with him this afternoon."

The señor replied with enraptured good will. "Ah," he said, "but the Mademoiselle's father is not arriving. The excursion of the father of the Mademoiselle has been cancelled."

Madeline sneered. But she searched his face and in a moment the sneer gave way to uncertain panic:

"You have talked to my father?"

The señor responded with his most engaging smile:

"Sí, Mademoiselle. Many times."

Madeline was stunned. For a time she sat trembling, poised on the edge of her chair as if awaiting explanation. Then her fists knotted at her sides, a quiver went through her body, and suddenly she pitched forward into the grass, moaning and twisting, beating her knuckles against her head. "You did this!" she cried. "Why? How much did you pay him for me?"

And she continued so, crying and pleading, as if already proof existed in support of this extravagant claim.

The señor vacated his lawn chair and strolled down to the pool where Don José had been idly standing for the past few minutes.

The dona, oblivious to Madeline's frenetic behaviour, returned a final time to collect and remove their dishes. Sr. Gómez sent Don José out to scratch beneath the rose bushes planted in triple rows at the lower end of the garden. He then withdrew into the casa to procure his white umbrella. The children of Manuel, who were allowed by their parents to enter the pool only when it was empty, ran up to timidly estimate the progress made that morning against the water—and ran away with contrived urgency a moment later when their mother called. Manuel could be seen pacing out a small plot of earth in the unbroken ground up from the path to the garbage dump—for here today with the señor's permission he and his wife were to plant the spinach and the tomatoes and the corn. . . and over there perhaps, why not, a new place where the pig might root to his satisfaction. . . for his was a decent family which held the señor's love and was not therefore required like the unfortunate poor to eat the leaf of the cactus all year long.

Madeline grappled back into her chair, there to mutter curses while scratching and slapping at her skin, separating blades of warm grass from her oiled body.

A few white clouds drifted in, momentarily screening out the sun.

Señor Gómez reappeared. For a time he passed aimlessly up and down his wide slate walk, the rolled umbrella swinging in energetic rhythm from his left hand. Several times he seemed determined to approach Madeline who was now softly weeping in her chair, though on each occasion some new thought seemed to impede him. Finally he contented himself by taking up a position under the shade of one of his most formidable trees, from which point he stared glumly across the lawn at his erubescent companion. His view was drawn particularly to Madeline's long red fingernails which he had ordered her to so paint soon after their first meeting. The colour in his opinion was altogether appropriate. Tiny pools of blood that had cooled and deepened—and which served at once to signal her value. The nails of all her predecessors had in fact been coloured the same. The blood of such women was infamous, symbolic of a thing so callous that he could see it always in his mind's eye, especially those late nights after Madeline had drunk herself past rancour and fatigue, past all attempts to fasten blame—those hours when she lay in his arms and all her whining delusions of supremacy were surrendered.

The señor did not pause to consider that at such times he lay in her arms with a similar calm, sharing in the advantages of that temporary truce. It would have displeased him vastly to consider that in their mutual pleasure they in any way significantly accommodated each other. Nor for that matter did the señor find it convenient to reflect on his own eccentric fascination with these *inglesas*, a fascination that was eccentric not because they were women or *inglesa* but because he harboured no equivalent scorn for their gringo compatriots. Were one to pursue with him the inevitable sequence of such reasoning he might have readily conceded that such sexual distinctions as frequently he was disposed to utter originated out of a most extreme bias. He might have agreed that the Mexican male's opinion of their women was not of the highest, and that on this account his guest had every reason to express fury. He would have pointed out, however, that Madeline had not the slightest concern for Mexico's women, and had failed even to notice their inequality.

He was content now to remain under his tree and dwell to his satisfaction on one aspect of the labyrinthine nature of these *inglesas*. It was perversely true, and a mystery past his ability to comprehend, that Mexico's sun was so terribly unkind to these visitors. They had a tendency to disappear when confronting the sun day after day in his garden. With great confidence they shed their clothing and surrendered themselves, thinking perhaps that one sun was so much like another. Their hair dulled, their eyes glazed, flesh slackened on their

154

bones. They became speckled and dirty, as if the sun sucked the filth out of them and left it to rot on their surface.

They reminded him, in fact, a bit of the El Flores dogs.

The señor's speculations along these lines were interrupted by the arrival at his door of an unfamiliar vendedor who happily announced the availability now of *la bonita fresas* and who held up two pails which had arrived he said that very day by autobús and which were for sale now *muy borato*, very cheap. The señor examined the strawberries with much delight, agreeing with the vendedor that they were indeed beautiful and at last instructing him to journey inside the casa where he might conclude arrangements with the dona. After numerous expressions of gratitude and remarks on the perfect weather, the man departed to fulfill this mission.

Waiting outside the señor's walls on the cobblestones of Calle de la Noche de la mil Lunas was yet another person desiring the señor's attention. Sighing, he noted there the familiar and insistent señora who lived in the hut behind the *mercado* now with her seven children and her dead husband whose mouth also would not be filled. Her wrinkled and dark Tarascan face with its fateful eyes was shrouded behind a mantilla and wrapped within the rebozo slung over her shoulder rested the inert form of her youngest child who might only be sleeping but who also might be dead. The señor advanced, realizing full well that the woman had nothing more to show him than her usual inconsequential and artless embroideries depicting, as she would herself tell him, the *bonito mucho bonito* rooster in the red thread or the blue and each such a good gift for the señor's white novia or such a practical aid to the señor's dona Anna when she wipes the dishes in the kitchen.

The señor refused her goods but gave her a twenty-peso note and suggested she visit him again in a few days when she might have for sale a serviette in the yellow.

He walked past Madeline—drawn up now with her head

between her knees—and returned to stand by the pool.

He heard her once shouting to him:

"You could have put chlorine in the goddamn water!" to which he silently replied that the Mademoiselle's chemicals would retard his garden and, moreover, had a disagreeable odour.

The rain came with its usual suddenness.

Madeline dashed across the garden, shrieking, and disappeared through the side wooden door.

The señor walked under his umbrella to where the lawn chairs were positioned, and with Don José's assistance, removed them to the shed where they were customarily stored and where they would now remain until tomorrow.

He walked with Don José out to the pool and together they stood on the white wall watching the rain spatter down and drum on the green surface. The rain was wondrously cool and thick—it seemed to whir through the air and ten feet in the distance one could see nothing—and the two exchanged pleasant remarks on this daily phenomenon, reminding each other repeatedly that tomorrow the garden would be even more beautiful.

Shortly afterward, his linen suit adhering to his thin frame, the señor turned leisurely through the side door and entered the casa to explain to the Mademoiselle the exact nature of his single dialogue with her father.

For half an hour it rained.

Then the sun again came out, as dazzling and as blistering as it had been before. Señora Pesuna emerged from the casa and went home to attend to her own many children. Don José, in the room where he had sought shelter, hunched on the floor and for some time investigated the condition of his shoes. Manuel and his family assembled by the path to the dump, from there proceeding to perform mysterious duties over the earth where their vegetables would be planted. Señor Gómez, if one knew where to look, would be found at his desk giving attention to one or the other of his numerous business affairs.

A light steam hovered loyally over the surface of the pool and for some hours the señor's beautiful garden remained empty. Eventually Madeline made her appearance and trudged still in her bathing suit down to the pool. She secured a long pole and with it attempted to separate the slime which the sun was already drying. A clearing barely large enough to accommodate her body was soon effected: she sat poised on the wall, closed her eyes, and slid gently into the water. She stretched face-down and for a moment floated there; then she kicked out from the wall and, so propelled, disappeared underwater.

From his window in the casa the señor watched her. Periodically her head broke through the green cover, her mouth gasped open; then again her head submerged, the legs shot through the water, the scum rearranged itself above her, and for another minute or so he would see nothing of her.

He was pleased with her, for the first time in his memory.

Copyright © 1977 by Leon Rooke

All rights reserved. No part of this book may be reproduced in any form or by any means, electronic or mechanical, except by a reviewer, who may quote brief passages in a review to be printed in a newspaper or magazine or broadcast on radio or television. "If Lost Return to the Swiss Arms" first appeared in the *Carolina Quarterly* and was an *O. Henry Awards* selection in 1965; "Leave Running" first appeared in *Epoch*, "If You Love Me Meet Me There" in the *University of Windsor Review*, "Memoirs of a Cross-country Man" in *Prism International*. "Call me Belladonna" first appeared in the *Antigonish Review* under the title "From the Love Parlour." "For Love of Madeline," "For Love of Eleanor" and "For Love of Gómez" were first published in *The Southern Review*.

These stories were selected for Oberon by John Metcalf.

ISBN 0 88750 231 8 (hardcover)
ISBN 0 88750 232 6 (softcover)

Cover etching, *Midnight Waltz*, by W. J. Wood, courtesy of the National Gallery of Canada, Ottawa

Design by Michael Macklem

PUBLISHED IN CANADA BY OBERON PRESS

Printed in Canada